perspective of his lifelong search for authentic spiritual truth.

I've had a variety of interactions with him, on-air and off. Every one of them has led to more meaningful thought and faithful belief.

Read his work, and enjoy the experience!

—Gary Stearman
Chief Executive Officer and Host,
*Prophecy Watchers*

L.A. Marzulli proves once again that he's not just a brilliant researcher, teacher, and writer when it comes to the supernatural—he also knows how to captivate readers with his compelling stories. Twenty years ago, his novel Nephilim sparked a similar passion within me. In *The Waiting Room*, L.A. explores the controversial yet well-documented phenomenon of near-death experiences, showing how God can use a traumatic event to change us completely. I hope you find L.A. Marzulli's storytelling talent as inspiring as I have.

—Derek Gilbert
Gilbert House Ministries
Author/Host of *Five in Ten*

Few ministers have walked into spiritual battle with the consistency and conviction of L.A. Marzulli. For years, he has reached those captive to unseen powers of deception and oppression—rescuing those trapped in New Age practices, breaking the grip of demonic influence, and helping the church discern the reality of fallen beings and end-times deception with biblical clarity. His ground-breaking ministry hasn't only shifted the trajectories of innumerable lives, but it has drawn people toward the redemption found in Christ alone.

—Joe Horn
CEO, SkyWatch TV and Defender Publishing

# THE WAITING ROOM

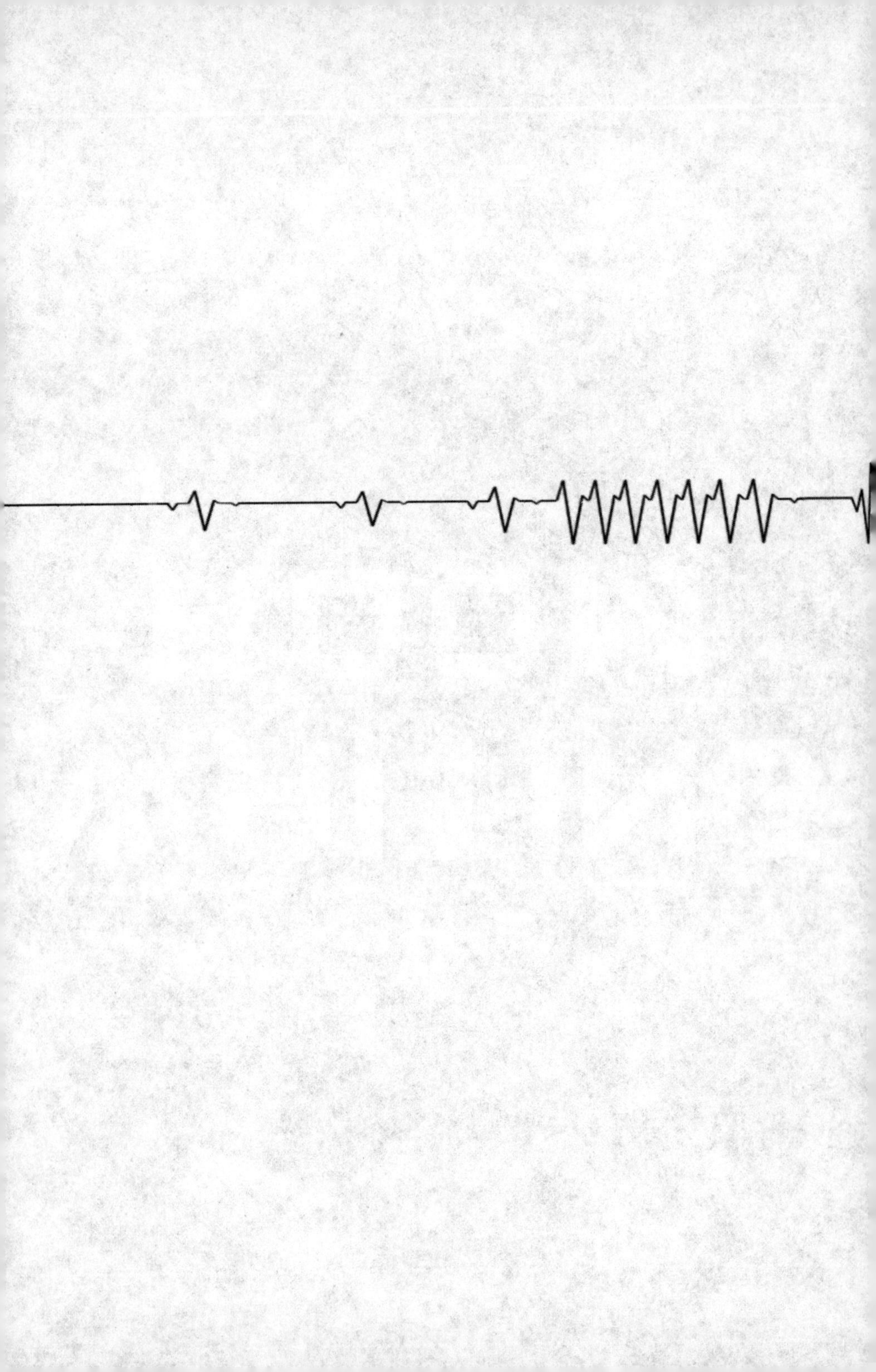

I cannot recommend *The Waiting Room* by L.A. Marzulli enough. He beautifully weaves together a gripping and raw story of faith, hope, forgiveness, and the glorious hope of life after this life. I was not able to put this book down and was brought, unexpectedly, to tears of joy and exhilaration at what God has planned for those that love Him. Some authors write historical fiction, but L.A. has written a future fiction, and you will be blessed by the message in this story.

—Mondo Gonzales<br>Cohost, *Prophecy Watchers*

L. A. Marzulli is at it again, using his skill as a wordsmith and storyteller to weave a tale with profound spiritual insights in an un-put-downable story of healing and redemption. *The Waiting Room* takes the reader on an incredible journey through life, death, and the transformational power of forgiveness. With its vivid encounters, cosmic powers, compelling characters, and profound themes, *The Waiting Room* is a transformative experience that will leave the reader with a sense of inspiration, renewal, and hope.

—Dr. Mark Conn<br>Pastor, Professor, Author,<br>Lecturer, Researcher

L.A. Marzulli's latest book, *The Waiting Room*, will take you on an insightful journey that emphasizes invaluable kingdom principles ranging from forgiveness and salvation to the captivating accounts of Satan's fall, the story of Adam and Eve, and even the Nephilim, all communicated in a way only he can. L.A. is a tremendous wordsmith with an uncanny ability to connect deep theological concepts with his riveting storytelling style. God has anointed the voice of Mr. Marzulli as much more than an intrepid host who uncovers some of the greatest discoveries of our generation—he also reaches beyond the barriers that many speakers and authors are unable to achieve. He offers engaging intrigue and answers for skeptics and seekers of truth alike.

L.A., you are one of the finest expositors of revelatory truth in our time. Thank you, sir, for opening the eyes of a generation to so many secrets and crucial knowledge that would otherwise be lost in a world attempting to go mad. It is my honor to endorse your latest work!

—Joseph Z
Author, Broadcaster, Prophetic Voice
JosephZ.Com

Few stories reach into the heart like *The Waiting Room*. It reminded me of my own moment of surrender, when I had to truly forgive my father as an adult—not just say the words but release the wound. That decision changed everything in me. This book beautifully reflects that same truth. Through a powerful near-death journey and a tender walk through defining moments, L. A. Marzulli shows us that forgiveness is not weakness—it is freedom. This story calls us to lay down old offenses, reconcile while we still have breath, and prepare our hearts for eternity.

—Larry Ragland
Pastor, Solid Rock Church
Author; Broadcaster; Host, *The Big Picture*

L. A. Marzulli is a longtime personal friend. For years, I have been a Christian writer and broadcaster, presenting the futurist worldview of events that point to the near fulfillment of Bible prophecy. He sees the present world as guided by God's own hand. In a very unique way, he writes manuscripts and produces videos that cover many of the same prophetic subjects I've brought to audiences everywhere.

It was on this foundation that our paths crossed years ago. We both believe that humankind lives in an important and dynamic historical period—most likely at the very end of the church age. This realization touches his imagination, emotions, and intellect in a unique and special way.

L.A. is moved by the depth and variety of great mysteries that bring us along the pathway of life, and the amazing

# THE WAITING ROOM

A NOVEL

L. A. MARZULLI

REALMS

The Waiting Room by L. A. Marzulli
Published by Realms, an imprint of Charisma Media
1150 Greenwood Blvd., Lake Mary, Florida 32746

For more resources like this, visit MyCharismaShop.com.

Cataloging-in-Publication Data is on file with the Library of Congress.
International Standard Book Number: 978-1-63641-571-0
E-book ISBN: 978-1-63641-572-7

1 2025
Printed in the United States of America

*I dedicate* The Waiting Room *to my Savior, who rescued this lost lamb over forty-five years ago. It is He who guides my steps and has delivered me from darkness and set my feet on solid ground.*

*And to Michelle Mintzer, who was tragically killed in an automobile accident when she was only sixteen years old. We met when she was fourteen, and she was my first real girlfriend, even though I was two years older than her.*

*Her death impacted me deeply, and I began to search for the meaning of life. If there was a God, why would He allow her untimely death?*

*Years later I found Jesus, or more realistically, He found me, rescued me, and put my feet on solid ground. He is the keeper of my soul and a light unto my path.*

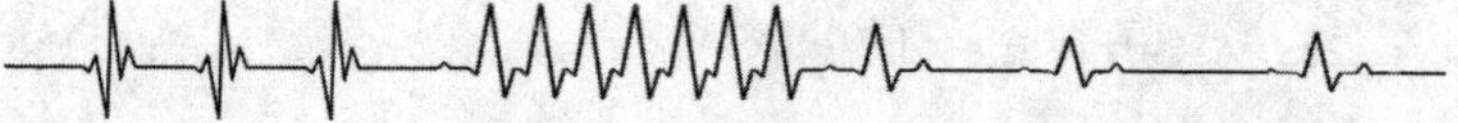

# CONTENTS

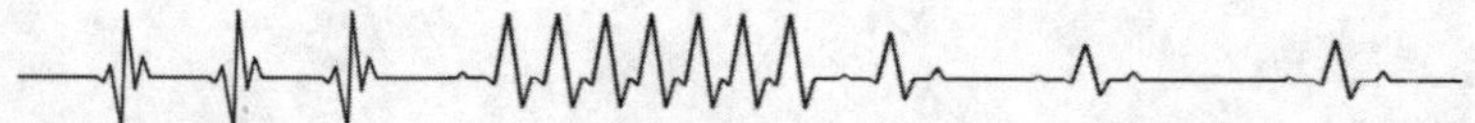

# A NOTE FROM THE AUTHOR

HAT YOU'RE ABOUT to read is in no way meant to be a blueprint for what happens when a person dies and crosses over. It is a work of fiction. However, I believe God is a God of second chances. And based on my own near-death experience and those of other people, it seems like some people get a second chance—and come back to earth changed, with a divine mission—while others continue on into heaven.

God is a loving God, and we don't know the depth of His love. Even after a person who's an atheist dies, could there be one more chance? We just don't know.

Ultimately, this book is a teaching tool. I encourage you to read it with an open heart. Remember, we all have free will—we can forgive, or we can hold on to bitterness. The choice is up to you and me.

# 1
# BIRD'S-EYE VIEW

I AM FLOATING ABOVE my bed in St. Thomas Hospital. It's really amazing. I'm looking down, and there I am in a hospital gown, lying on the bed with my eyes closed, tubes and wires sticking out of me and connected to beeping monitors. I look like something out of a Frankenstein movie. Evelyn, my wife of forty years, is sitting comatose on an uncomfortable hospital chair in the corner of the room, with the crossbar digging into the middle of her back. Our son is next to her on a clone of the uncomfortable chair. He's not paying attention to her. He's on his cell phone answering yet another one of the endless texts that keep his generation from living in the present.

Oh, well. I like it up here at the ceiling; I have a bird's-eye view of what's going on. I love to fly, and this is it. I'm flying!

I was a commercial airline pilot for over thirty years and loved every flight I captained. My dad had a Stearman airplane, and I remember when I was five years old, sitting next to him as he gave me my first flying lesson. By eight years old, I could fly solo, but of course Dad would not allow that. So here I am *really* flying at last, and I'm loving it. But how does this work?

I can see that I'm attached to my body by some kind of

silver cord. Wait—I've read about this somewhere. Isn't that in the Bible? The silver cord? No matter, I'm enjoying my lofty perch. Yet I am somewhat disturbed at seeing my motionless body lying there below me—my face ashen, my eyes closed, my cheeks sunken. And I mentioned the wires, monitors, and fluids that are working overtime to keep me alive. I'm not dead—yet. But here I am, floating, flying. This is really cool! I can see my heartbeat on the monitor. It looks pretty good; maybe I'll pull through. On the other hand, this is really amazing. Why haven't other people talked about this? Maybe they have.

As I float down to the floor, I'm about two feet away from my wife's face. Dear Evelyn. She's been crying. Her eyes are closed, and she's clutching a tissue in her right hand. My scatterbrained son is still on his cell phone, seemingly oblivious to the drama going on around him.

"Hey, Phil!" I yell with everything inside me. "Hey, Phil… you idiot! Can't you see that your mom needs you? Hello in there!"

Part of me expects Evelyn and Phil to hear or see me, but they don't. What's really strange is that I can see through the walls in the room as if they're transparent. I see them shimmer as I look over at the woman in the room next to me. She's propped up in her bed, watching something on TV. Welcome to hospital life. There's nobody with her. She's alone except for the idiot box that has 800 channels and nothin' on. Isn't that a lyric from a song?

I find I can actually float—no, fly—through the walls. But this silver cord attached to my body lets me go only so far and then *yank*, like a dog being chained to its doghouse, and I can go no farther. How does that work? Still, it's a wonderful feeling to be able to fly around. I'm having fun even though my body below me seems to be giving out.

Back to Evelyn.

We've been married…how long? I think it's been forty years.

Or is it forty-one? I suppose I can do the math, but I have trouble adding up the bogies, double bogies, and triple bogies on my golf card, so I'm just going to go with forty years of marital bliss. A nice round number. I'm being facetious. It's been good. But like all marriages, there have been potholes in the road. Three kids, one miscarriage, the death of our middle child at the tender age of nine—which very nearly led to a divorce—and a partridge in a pear tree when Evelyn built an aviary in our backyard. Her love for her feathered friends was unwavering; I am somewhat jealous. It was her way of coping with our loss. I think a mother's love for a child is something a man will never fully grasp.

Evelyn's shoulder-length gray hair is disheveled. She's been camped out in my hospital room for three days. And no makeup. Normally she wouldn't go anywhere without her lipstick. Her shoulders are hunched over, and her face is tearstained.

Seeing her this way has made me lose some of my excitement for being outside my body and flying around the hospital corridors.

Phil is still scrolling on his cell.

Where is my daughter? Why isn't she here? What about Fred—my best friend from college—and also our pastor? Why isn't he here?

I fly back up to the ceiling and wonder how long this will take. I'm not hungry. I'm not tired. I'm not sick anymore. I'm all here, and I'm flying.

I can see down the hallway. The elevator doors open and out comes a woman with purple hair. Even though the elevator and the woman who just exited from it are about forty yards away, I know it's my daughter, Marsha. How can I put this in a politically correct way? We are estranged. We are about as far apart as two people can be. Evelyn and I often lament how we lost her. Where did we go wrong?

When we sent her off to college, she was an innocent

eighteen-year-old girl with long blonde hair and a smile that could light up a room. She'd had many boyfriends all through high school but never got serious. She sang in the church choir. By the spring of that year—her first year in college—she was a different person. Evelyn and I hardly recognized her. She had chopped all her hair off, shaved one side of her head, and dyed the rest of her hair purple. Evelyn did her best to choke back the tears, but I was irate. "What…why did you do this?" I barked.

I won't go into the brief time she was with us during spring break, but one bomb after another was dropped on us. She had a girlfriend, and they were "in love." Marsha was a sophomore, and this girlfriend was a senior. It was she—whose name I will not mention—that groomed Marsha. It took only from Christmas to spring break. Marsha was someone I no longer knew and—I hate to admit—no longer loved.

At least she didn't bring "the one I will not name" with her. That's all Evelyn would need now.

I watch as Marsha makes her way to the room, wearing her newly adopted college uniform: baggy pants and a T-shirt with a rainbow-colored Che Guevara on it; one arm tatted up; an unlit cigarette tucked behind her ear; and, of course, the patch of purple weeds that is left of her hair.

Oh, wait. I forgot about the earbuds blasting who knows what into the empty space between her ears. As she half-dances her way up the hallway to my room, she is lip-synching to the song—or whatever it is—blasting in her head that keeps her in her own little fantasy world.

I decide to head her off, so I fly down toward her and get in her face.

"Hey, Marsha! Hi. Hello in there."

She walks right through me, as if I'm not even there. In reality, I suppose I'm not.

I follow her into my room.

What I see next surprises me—no, shocks me. Marsha takes

one look at me lying comatose—ashen, half dead—and her hands fly up to cover her face as she breaks into uncontrollable sobs.

Evelyn jumps out of her chair, throwing her arms around Marsha, and the two of them weep on each other's shoulders.

Phil is jolted out of his cellphone utopia and stands up but doesn't know what to do. Phil and Marsha are at odds with each other too, so all this is complex, and it's not going to get fixed in five minutes.

"Is he dying?" Marsha blurts out.

Evelyn nods slightly. "It appears that way. But anything is possible with God."

At that Marsha "snaps" out of it. "Please don't bring *Him* into this. Why would He allow such a thing? Dad's been healthy all his life, and now he's at death's door? I don't get it. It's not fair. I'm sure you're saying your prayers, and I can see they're really working for you." She takes a step back from Evelyn—having got hold of her true self—and the purple persona is back.

"Look at him," Marsha says without filtering. "He's dying, for Chri—"

"Don't you dare say that!" Evelyn's hackles are up. "How dare you take His name in vain at a time like this."

"Way to go, Evie." My nickname for her. "Don't take any wooden nickels."

Evie loves church, loves the choir, loves Sunday morning, loves telling people about Jesus. Me, not so much. I mean, I'm a Christian. But I've never seen a miracle, never been healed of anything, even the common cold. Never felt the presence of the Holy Spirit, whatever that is. All in all, I am what my good friend Fred—or rather Pastor Fred—calls me. I'm a CEO: Christmas and Easter Only, and that works for me. I chuckle to myself.

"OK, sorry," Purple-Hair mutters under her breath.

Now it's Phil's turn. "You know, you come here like you're

going to a club or something, and you're not here for two minutes before you and Mom are going at it. Don't you give a flip about anyone but yourself?"

Look who's calling the kettle black. "Hey, Phil!" I bark. "Thanks for putting down your stupid slave box and actually engaging in reality for once." Stinking cell phones.

Phil takes a step toward Marsha, but before he can say or do anything, Marsha raises her hand and whacks the cell phone out of Phil's hand, sending it crashing to the floor.

"What the..." Phil stammers as he picks up the phone, which has a cracked glass screen. "What the..."

Evie glares at Marsha. "I can't believe you just did that."

Marsha shrugs, turns away, and plops down in one of the chairs.

As if on cue, Fred comes into the room. We met as roommates in college, and it was Fred who led me to Jesus during our senior year—after endless debates on who Jesus was. What ultimately convinced me was a book Fred gave me about the Shroud of Turin. When he presented it to me, I scoffed and blurted out that it was Middle Ages forgery.

"Not so fast, citizen!" Fred countered. "You don't know anything about the shroud; that's ignorance on your part. And the fact that you're saying you do is arrogance. They are a deadly combination." And with that he placed the book in my hand. Three weeks later, I came across the line, and with Fred's help I asked Jesus into my heart. The book on the shroud had convinced me of the resurrection; I was sold. However, unlike Fred, I didn't really fit into church life and became what Fred called me: a CEO—Christmas and Easter Only.

"Evelyn, Phil...Marsha," Fred says, touching each person as he moves through the room toward my bed. "How long has he been like this?"

"Three days, and he's fading," Evelyn says, softly. "It's not looking good. The doctors say they've done all they can do." She stifles a sob.

Fred touches my forehead and lets his hand rest there. I can see he's praying, but—out of respect for Phil, who's become a staunch atheist, and, of course, Marsha—he doesn't fill the room with the verbiage of a prayer.

Marsha shifts her weight.

Phil scrolls on his phone, though the cracked glass makes it hard for him to read the most recent text.

Fred is from Texas, and even after all the years of living in our little community in Southern California, he still has the Texas twang. I never tire of kidding him about it.

He slowly pulls his hand from my forehead, and I can see he is tearing up.

Whispering to Evelyn, he says, "We'll see what the Lord can do. It's not over yet."

A loud warning sound erupts on one of the monitors.

All eyes focus on the machine.

A nurse runs into the room.

Then another nurse.

Fred and Evelyn move out of the way and stand on the sidelines of the action.

"He's flatlining," I hear one of the nurses say.

Two men come in with some sort of paddle-like things in their hands.

"Just in time," one of the nurses blurts out as she and the other nurse expose my chest while the men get ready.

I realize that my heart has stopped beating. I've seen this in movies for I don't know how long. They're going to try to restart my heart.

"Clear!" one of the men yells.

I hear a whizzing sound and then *bang!* I go sailing across the room into the hallway.

"Hey! I felt that!" I yell, wondering how this is possible.

A doctor rushes in, brushing by my family and Fred, and is overseeing the action.

"Anything?" he asks, looking at the monitor.

"Not yet. Clear!" The man with the paddles shouts again as he gives me another shock, sending me sailing down the hallway.

I fly back into the room and watch the action below me. And then it happens.

I hear a deep, rushing sound, like a huge wave about to break on the beach. I feel something snap, and looking down, I see that the silver cord has detached itself from my body.

Like a human cannonball, I'm flying out of the hospital so fast that the city below me disappears in a flash.

I'm headed toward a point of light beyond the atmosphere, and seconds later I have entered what appears to be a tunnel of light. The walls are like golden glass, but I can see through them as I fly through the universe. How can this be? Planets are whizzing by me. Stars and galaxies grow large and then disappear as I continue this incredible journey.

Suddenly I have a sensation of falling, and the golden tunnel has disappeared.

"Am I in heaven?" I wonder.

An overwhelming silence and a peaceful stillness enfold me.

# 2
# MEETING MR. O

I AM LITERALLY SPEECHLESS, as the trip here has been…well, I can't exactly describe it. I was flying through the universe at…what speed? I don't know. I only know that one moment I was hovering above the hospital bed watching the monitor flatline. Then all the commotion with the nurses and doctors happened, Evie became hysterical—and the cord snapped, sending me flying through…the universe? The astral plane? Whatever this is…the second heaven? Hey! How many heavens are there anyway?

Nevertheless, here I am in a room…somewhere. I'm real, and I'm here, but I don't know where I am.

There are no windows, but there is a door. It's a beautifully carved door with abalone inlays of birds in flight. Stunning.

The carpet looks like it came out of a museum. It's plush, and my feet sink into it. The lighting…where is the light coming from? There are no light bulbs or fixtures—it's just here. How does that work? There is a long table in front of me, and it appears to be an antique with carved legs and a three-inch-thick top, whose planks have been dovetailed together with a darker wood—walnut maybe? I don't know.

I look back at the door and notice there's no handle on it. Strange.

There's a knock on the door. Before I can say anything, it opens and in comes a man who looks like a cross between Doc in the *Back to the Future* movie and Albert Einstein.

I'm taken aback, wondering what will happen next.

"Mr. Frisbee?" he asks, looking up at me through wire-rimmed glasses. "Bob Frisbee?"

"Yes, and where am I anyway? And who are you?"

The man clears his throat, adjusts his glasses, and lowers his head. "You're in the Waiting Room, and I'm Mr. Olam, but you can call me Mr. O for short. I'm here to help you through the next phase of…well, you'll understand in a bit or two."

"A bit or two," I repeat, sarcastically, frowning.

"Why don't you take a seat, make yourself comfortable, and I'll try to explain."

I pull out one of the chairs with an embroidered cushion back and settle myself into it, noticing how unexpectedly comfortable it is.

"Are you comfortable?" Mr. O asks, a slight smile creasing his face.

"Yes, thank you," I reply, wondering whether this guy is reading my mind. "Where am I? I thought I was supposed to be with Jesus if I died. Isn't that what the Bible tells us?"

Mr. O adjusts his glasses again and sits down across from me at the table. "How do you know you're not?"

"You don't look anything like His picture."

"Really? And what does He look like?"

I stare at Mr. O for a beat and then shrug my shoulders. "OK, I guess I really don't know."

"Well, let's get into it, shall we? The sooner we deal with all this, the sooner you'll be out of the Waiting Room."

"Wait just a minute here! Is this…what do Catholics call it…purgatory or something?"

"Absolutely not. Purgatory is an invention of man; it never has and never will exist, period," he says evenly, with an air of authority.

I try to gather my thoughts. "Then what is this? Where am I?"

"I told you. It's the Waiting Room. Oh, and by the way, time as you know it no longer exists. So we can take as long as you'd like to get through this."

"Get through what?"

Ignoring me, he asks, "Well then, should we just dive in?"

"Dive in?"

Mr. O reaches into his coat pocket and pulls out some sort of gold, metallic-looking object. He waves his hand over it, and a golden wheel at least six feet in diameter appears, its many spokes shooting out from the center. And to my astonishment, there is a portrait of me, Bob Frisbee, in the center, smiling. It's actually a good picture. I appear to be about thirty years old—much younger than my current age of sixty.

I follow one of the spokes from the center to the perimeter of the wheel. As I do so, I see faces appearing at the end of each spoke: all people I've known throughout my lifetime.

"Hey," I say, "that's Ms. Bittner, my first-grade teacher! I was always fond of her. She was a kind woman." This spoke on the wheel is lit brightly. But right next to it is another spoke, and it's dark. It has a picture of a young kid with an angry expression. He was the bully who pushed me up against the lockers outside Ms. Bittner's class.

"Why are some spokes lit up and others are not?" I ask.

"Good, very observant on your part," Mr. O says. "The lit-up spokes are people you love, people you have blessed throughout your life. The dark spokes are the people you've never forgiven."

"From the first grade?"

"Yes. Here, I'll show you how this works. All you have to do is bless David."

"How did you know his name?"

"I've read your file, and it's in there." Mr. O pats the large folder next to him with papers spilling out onto the table.

"Why do I have to…bless him? He was the bully! And after he pushed me against the locker, I knocked his two front teeth out." I smile slightly at that last thought.

"Yes, good for you; you won the fight. But you harbored ill will toward him for the rest of your life."

"I never thought about him after that."

"Yes," Mr. O points out, "but the scar is there, and it festered."

"Yes, but I never thought—"

"The spoke is dark, and that's not good. Look at it this way. What if you run into David up here? Then what?"

"What!? How would I recognize him after all these years?" I say dismissively.

"You would recognize him. Trust me, that's the way all this works up here."

"So what am I supposed to do? It's been decades since this happened!"

"You have to write a thousand times in longhand, *David, I forgive you.*"

"What? You must be kidding me!"

Mr. O lets out a laugh that fills the room with light—light that changes into birds in flight that then disappear. This snaps me to attention as I marvel at how that happened.

"I'm just playing with you." Mr. O smiles. "All you have to do is bless David. Simple, isn't it? If it was any harder, human beings couldn't do it."

I frown and wonder how this will work. "This is heaven? Seriously?"

"Well, yes and no. It's the Waiting Room."

"So what do I do? How can I *bless* David, someone I haven't seen in decades?"

Looking over his glasses at me, Mr. O says, "Do you know what the definition of the word *bless* is?"

"Think a happy thought toward the person? I don't really know."

"Well, here is the definition: *bless*—to invoke divine care for. And here's my favorite." He smiles as he extends his arms wide. "To confer prosperity or happiness upon. That's it!"

Somewhat annoyed, I ask, "So how do I do this? Why do I have to do this? How can this possibly affect David after all these years?"

"It's not about David. It's about lighting up the dark spokes on your wheel."

I fold my arms in front of my chest and glare at Mr. O. "Do I have any other choices here?"

He leans back in his chair and mimics me by folding his arms. "There's always what we call the Escape Tunnel."

"What's that?"

"Well, I'm not going to tell you yet. We're just starting to get underway. Perhaps you'll find out in due time."

"Look," I say, exasperated, "I want to know what's really going on. I don't get this at all. It seems like a tremendous waste of time."

"I told you, time doesn't exist here, as you know it. So from your perspective, we have all the time in the world to sort these things out."

Frowning again, I ask, "So how do I *bless* someone I haven't seen or honestly even thought of in years? What difference does it make?"

Mr. O unfolds his arms, and his eyes twinkle as he leans in toward me. "That last sentence you uttered—'What difference does it make?'—was also stated by one of your politicians when, in reality, it made all the difference on earth. And it does here too."

"I can't believe this," I mutter to myself. "David from the first grade?"

"Yes, David," Mr. O says, flatly.

"Hey! Are you reading my mind? How did you do that?"

Mr. O uses his index finger to push his glasses from falling off his nose and deliberately avoids my question.

"So what about David? Will you bless him? Will you confer happiness upon him or not?"

"I really have no choice here, do I?"

Mr. O is motionless in his chair with his eyes fixed on me. His eyes are almost like orbs of burning fire, and yet I sense what I can only call an overwhelming—dare I use the term *holy*—love burning for me. How is that possible? I only just arrived. Yet he does have the file, so I suppose he's read up on me, which brings up a whole list of other *situations* like the one with David that I don't want to face at the moment. But then, as Mr. O said, "Time doesn't exist here," so at some point I have a feeling—of dread—that he's going to address these things.

"So?" Mr. O asks again.

"OK," I say, resigned, "so what do I do?"

"Bless David. Say out loud, 'David, I forgive you and bless you and confer happiness upon you.'"

I take a deep breath and repeat what Mr. O has instructed me to say.

"Good," he says, "now look at the wheel."

I look over at the golden wheel, somehow floating in space, and see a faint glow next to Ms. Bittner's golden spoke.

"Why is it so faint?"

"Well, the wheel is able to measure your sincerity."

"What? How is that possible?"

"It's fairly technical, but the wheel measures your breathing, eye movement, body language, and rise in electrical current from your brain and heart."

Frowning again, I say, "My heart?"

"Yes, your heart. The wheel knows the intentions of your heart, and you're giving this 'blessing' a halfhearted attempt. Sorry, no pun intended."

Mr. O cracks himself up, but I'm not having any of it.

"Do you want to try again?" he asks. "By the way, you can't fake this. Let me help you."

"I'm ready. How are you going to help me?"

"Do you remember when you were in high school and your best friend Fred, who later became a pastor, hit you by mistake when the two of you were goofing around with karate kicks?"

I laugh, remembering how we thought we were Bruce Lee as teenagers, and Fred let go a wild kick that caught me in the solar plexus, and down I went.

"Yes, I remember. How did you… That's in the file?"

"Well, you forgave him instantly, didn't you?" He ignores my question, waiting for my reply.

"Yes, but he was, and is, my best friend."

"True, but that's what you have to do with David."

I mull over what Mr. O. said.

"Blessings and goodwill to David," he adds with enthusiasm. "You can do it! You've got this."

This guy is like a cosmic cheerleader. Except I'm realizing that after all these years, if I look deep enough, I still harbor ill will toward David. This happened so long ago—it really is a distant memory—yet I realize that it has—how did Mr. O put it?—*festered* in me for decades.

"OK, I think I get this."

"Good, so bless David with goodwill."

"Can I close my eyes?"

"If you think that will help, then go ahead and do it, but it's not necessary."

I close my eyes and take a deep breath.

"David…I say to you, blessings and goodwill."

I open one eye and glance at the wheel, and to my amazement the spoke is lighting up! I watch fascinated as the light beam travels up the spoke of the wheel. When it hits David's face, his angry expression turns into a radiant smile.

"Wow! That's incredible."

"You've got the hang of it," Mr. O says, "but we'll see how it goes from here."

# 3
# THE FILE

Mr. O is sorting through my file and turning the pages. "Hmm, what do we have here?"

I lean over to try to take a look at what he's holding, but Mr. O pulls back the pages in his hands so I can't see what he's looking at. "No peeking," he says sternly. But I can see that he's blustering; he's having fun with all this.

"So do you remember this?" he asks as he puts down on the table what looks like a Polaroid picture from the sixties.

I study it for a few seconds, and then a frown displaces the smile. "Isn't that my neighbor's house?"

Mr. O nods his head and says, "Watch this."

As I'm staring at the picture, it suddenly comes to life.

"Hey…how is this working?"

Mr. O points to the picture. "Just watch."

I can see the house where I grew up as a kid, and then to my amazement, I see myself walking across my backyard with my slingshot in my hand.

"That's me!"

"Mm-hmm." Mr. O nods in agreement.

It's almost getting dark, and the sun is about to set. I see myself go to the end of our yard and hop over the fence that separates our yard from our grouchy neighbor, Ms. La Farge. I see myself darting behind the trees in her yard as I get closer to the rear of her house.

"How does this work? How is it possible you have…what…a film of this? How?"

"Trust me, we have everything you've ever done." Mr. O points back to the moving picture. "Focus, please."

I know what's about to happen, but I am transfixed on the screen. I want to look away, but I keep staring at the scene unfolding before me. I feel a rush of nausea, of nervousness, well up inside me.

I watch myself, a boy of eight, hiding behind the trees as I get closer and closer to Ms. La Farge's house.

It's getting darker.

I sprint to the last tree in her yard, and now there's grass underfoot. I see myself pull a marble out of my pants pocket and insert it into the pocket of my slingshot. Before me is a large picture window fewer than thirty feet away.

I watch as the eight-year-old Bobby Frisbee pulls back the slingshot a few times and takes aim. He lets go and then *crash!* I hear and see the explosion of glass.

A devilish smile erupts on my young face. "Yes!" the fiendish boy says as he runs away. I see him hop the fence and then hide his…my…slingshot under some leaves at the base of a tree. Then the boy, me, Bobby Frisbee, slowly walks back into my boyhood home as if nothing has happened.

The postcard screen goes black.

Mr. O looks at me. "Well?"

I shift in my chair and push the picture back across the table toward him.

"I was just a kid. And besides, she was a nasty old bitty. She kept my baseball just because it went into her yard."

"Really?"

"Yes, and other stuff as well. None of us kids liked her."

"Are you trying to justify your actions?"

"No, but I'm only an eight-year-old kid! How can I be held, what…accountable?"

Mr. O reaches over and touches the photo. "Look again at this, please." He touches the card with his index finger, and the screen lights up again. I see—in slow motion—my face grinning in boyhood satisfaction as the window is shattered into pieces. Mr. O somehow zooms in, so I see a close-up of my face.

"Enjoying yourself?"

I shrug.

"Ms. La Farge called the police, and the police went to your house and talked with your parents. Do you remember what happened?"

"That was so long ago." I slide my feet needlessly.

"Do you remember? The police came. And what happened next?"

I fidget in my chair. "They asked me if I broke the window."

"And?"

I shift more in the chair. "I told them…I didn't break the window."

"What happened next?"

My foot starts bobbing up and down. "Well, the next day Ms. La Farge knocked on our door, and for some reason I answered it, not knowing it was her. She had the marble in her hand."

"What did she say?"

Squirming, I let out a sigh. "She said, 'Here's your marble.'"

"And?"

"She just turned around and walked away."

"So you got away with it."

"Yes, I suppose so."

"And you thought you were justified?"

I scowl as I cross my arms over my chest. "Yes, she was mean."

"Let me show you something."

Mr. O takes the metal thingy out of his coat pocket again. With a wave of his hand, a type of window opens—a portal that is looking back into the past.

"What am I looking at?"

"Ms. La Farge when she was a young girl."

I look closer and see a town that doesn't look like anything in the USA.

"Where is this?" I ask.

"The year is 1942, and you're looking at a small village in France. The young girl you see is Gina La Farge."

I watch as soldiers on tanks and motorcycles ride into the center of the village. I see the Nazi flags, the German helmets, and the swastikas on the uniforms. I watch as they round up people. The scene shifts, and I see Gina being herded into a truck with others. The trucks pull out of the town square.

"What's going on?" I ask, not yet comprehending.

"Watch."

I see the trucks pull into a camp surrounded by barbed-wire fences, with guard towers and soldiers patrolling the perimeters.

I see Gina La Farge step off the back of the truck along with the others. They are herded into the camp.

"What did she do that led to this?"

Mr. O replies in a steady and grave tone. "Her family was hiding Jews in their house. Remember, the Nazis killed over six million Jews—this was the Holocaust. The Nazis got wind of it when a neighbor informed them, and then the SS came."

Mr. O pauses for a second before continuing. "They shot her parents and others right before her eyes. But they took Gina to a camp. She remained there until the end of the war, and then she emigrated to America. She never really recovered from those events. She was raped by the guards. When she resisted them raping her, she was beaten and starved. She never married. She lived alone with her horrible memories. She worked at a bank, and by the time you knew her, she had retired. She was alone, bitter, and filled with hatred toward the men who had killed her parents and raped her."

Stunned, I stammer, "I…I had no idea."

"She was a bitter woman for whom laughter was like a dead, foreign language."

"I had no idea," I repeat, quietly.

Mr. O is staring at me.

"What am I supposed to do with this…now?"

"You shouldn't have done what you did, and you shouldn't have lied," he says pointedly.

"Is there a dark spoke in the wheel?"

"Yes. It's here." Mr. O points to the place on the wheel.

The wheel is very dark here, and at the far end of the spoke I can barely make out Ms. La Farge's picture. She has a very stern look.

"What now?"

"This is a bit complex, but you must repent of your actions. You must repent of the lie you told. You must repent of the hatred and bitterness you hold in your heart toward her."

"I don't hold hatred toward her!"

"You broke her window."

"That's not hating, is it?"

"Well, what do you think? It was a violent act, yes?"

Arms folded, I slouch down in my chair.

"I had no idea. If I had known, I never would have…"

"Exactly. That is the point. Everyone has a story. Some people wear it on their sleeve; others try to hide it. People are repositories for the garbage of the human race. Victims of the atrocities that human beings do to one another. Some, like Gina, never heal. They are stuck in time, frozen, incapable of healing themselves, and they sink deeper into their own pain until it consumes them. *If they would come to me, I would heal them.*"

Where have I heard that last statement before? What is Mr. O trying to say, and what is my part here? I wonder.

He continues, "To light up this spoke of the wheel, you have to bless Gina. But you also have to confess, admit, proclaim, come to grips with, realize, face, and examine to the fullest your actions, your thoughts, and your intentions toward Gina."

"Wow, that's a mouthful. How do I do that? This is impossible."

"Not really. You can do this; it's easy. Trust me. I've been through this many times, and it gets easier as you go. You know what to say, the blessing and goodwill part."

Shifting in my chair and looking down at the table to avoid Mr. O's gaze, I say, "I can do that, but what about…the lying?"

"Well, you can't erase your actions. But you can admit you were wrong and then ask for forgiveness. A better word for it is to repent of your actions—to turn away from what you did."

I can't believe this is happening. I haven't thought about Ms. La Farge for decades. And if I'm honest, when the slingshot incident comes to the forefront of my memory, which is a rarity, it brings a smile to my face.

"You're smirking," Mr. O says with an edge of sternness. "You see how these actions linger in your soul? Even when you think they're not there, they're part of you. They color your personality and make up who you are."

"I've never thought of it like that."

"Exactly. Most people don't. But what you do on earth stays with you—in some ways, for all eternity—if not checked."

"Checked?"

"Yes, like what you did with David. You have to deal with this now, because what would happen if you ran into Ms. La Farge up here?"

"She's here?"

"Yes."

I am taken aback by this and wonder how an old bitty like

Ms. La Farge could be here—in heaven! This doesn't seem like heaven; it's more like an inquisition. Mr. O is like a heavenly Savonarola, if there is such a thing.

He continues, "Can you find it in your heart and soul to bless her and ask for forgiveness?"

I'm staring at the picture again, trying to find a way out.

After a moment of silence, he adds, "There's always the Escape Tunnel, but I don't think you're ready for that yet."

I wonder what the *Escape Tunnel* is, and I involuntarily shudder, not knowing why.

"What if I don't want to?"

Mr. O gets up from the table. "Then we'll wait." Without another word he takes a step toward the door, and then he turns and asks, "Are you sure?"

I don't like the sound of that. "I'm not sure of anything at this point."

"Well then?"

"OK, OK. I'll do it," I mumble, barely audible.

Mr. O takes his place directly across from me.

I look over at the wheel, then reach out and touch it. My hand reflects the golden rays that light the wheel, but as I move my hand toward Ms. La Farge's spoke, the light vanishes, and with it so does my hand, as a black shadow blots out all the light.

This is unsettling.

I sigh. "OK, I bless Ms. La Farge. I bless her. I *bless* her, and I'm sorry for what I did."

Something happens unexpectedly that I'm not at all ready for. I find myself sobbing, my shoulders shaking. As I'm crying, I say, repeatedly, "I'm sorry…I'm so sorry…I'm sorry."

"Look at the wheel," Mr. O says, pointing at it.

The spoke that just a moment ago was dark is now lit up! As I go to the end of it, where the picture of Ms. La Farge had been,

I see in its place a picture of a smiling young girl whom I realize was her before the bad things happened to her.

I take a breath as I wipe my eyes with the sleeve of my shirt. "You said she was here?"

"Yes, would you like to see her?" Mr. O asks.

"Now?"

"Why not?"

"I don't think I'm ready for that. Can I take a rain check on it? I mean…all this…that's happening is just…so overwhelming. Later, OK?"

"As you wish." Mr. O waves his hand in front of him, as if I'm a king or something.

"Isn't that from *The Princess—*"

"*Bride*!" He laughs as he says the last part before I can finish. "Yes! As you wish, but there's more we need to look at."

"You watched *The Princess Bride*?"

"The Dread Pirate Roberts has come for your soul!" Mr. O says, sounding just like Fezzik the Giant.

"Seriously?" I crack up as I wipe the last traces of tears from my face.

And with that Mr. O returns to the large folder while glancing at the wheel floating in space.

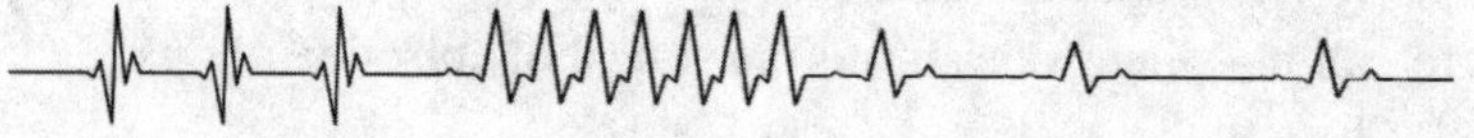

# 4
# THE WAY-BACK MACHINE

ELL, WHAT DO we have here?" Mr. O removes some pages from his folder.

Under my breath, I mutter, "I can only imagine."

Mr. O ignores me. "You're doing really well. You've got this!"

He is acting as my cheerleader. But I'm still somewhat in shock from the last spoke I had to deal with, so again I mutter, "*I can only imagine.*"

"Let's go to your sixth-grade class."

"Do we have to?"

"Of course we do. We have to get all the spokes in your wheel to light up." He smiles as he gestures to the floating wheel. "This is an easy one."

I'm not buying the "easy" part at all.

Mr. O turns the pages. "Here it is. Mrs. Clavanese."

"No. This can't be happening. How did you…never mind, I get it. You know all, see all," I say sarcastically as my hands provide emphasis.

"That's 110 percent true. Now to Mrs. Clavanese. Do you want to watch in the Way-Back Machine?"

"Wait, now you're referencing the *Rocky and Bullwinkle* show?"

"Yes, one of your favorites. I pay special attention to detail."

"Are you talking about the video thingy—I don't know what to call it—when we watched the slingshot episode?"

"Exactly!"

I lean forward, and I'm smirking a little. Mr. O knows the right buttons to push. "Is it really called the Way-Back Machine?" I'm almost whispering.

"Well, for you it is."

I let out a mischievous laugh. "Let's watch then."

With a wave of his hand, the video starts, and I'm transfixed. There I am, so long ago.

"The picture is really good, but can you turn up the sound a little?"

"Seriously?" Mr. O peers at me.

I watch. I'm sitting all the way in the back of the class—in the middle of the room. Mrs. Clavanese is standing before the class and speaking.

"I want to let all of you students know that you did a very good job with the latest art projects you participated in. I want to hold up a picture that caught the art teacher's eye, as well as mine."

Mrs. Clavanese holds up the picture. "Craig, you did a wonderful job on this picture. Congratulations."

Craig is the teacher's pet. He shifts uncomfortably in his chair. "I didn't draw that."

The teacher looks taken aback. "What? Are you sure?"

"Yes, ma'am."

"Well then, class, who drew this incredible picture?"

"Wait for it," Mr. O whispers.

I see myself tentatively raise my hand. "I did."

Mrs. Clavanese's face wrinkles, showing her immediate disapproval. "Bobby Frisbee? You did this?"

"Yes, ma'am."

"Are you sure?"

"Yes, Mrs. Clavanese."

"You wouldn't be taking someone else's work…like Craig's… and taking credit for it, would you?

"No, Mrs. Clavanese."

"So you drew this without anyone's help?'

"Yes, Mrs. Clavanese."

"Are you sure, Bob Frisbee?"

"Yes, ma'am."

"Did your mother help with this?"

"No, Mrs. Clavanese."

"Mr. Frisbee, lying has consequences, so I'm assuming you wouldn't be lying to the entire class, now, would you?"

"No, Mrs. Clavanese."

"I'll ask you one last time. Did you draw this picture by yourself without any help?" She pauses. "Did Craig help you?"

"No, Mrs. Clavanese."

"No? So you did have help?

"That's not what I meant to say. No, Craig didn't help, and nobody else did either. I just drew it by myself."

Mrs. Clavanese folds her arms in front of her, which creases my art paper, and walks down the aisle and places the picture on my desk. "A C+ for you, Mr. Frisbee."

The class all laughs in unison.

I see myself staring at my desk. I realize that I'm powerless. Mrs. Clavanese holds all the cards. She makes the rules. And in this instant, I see that the great picture she thought was Craig's has been reduced to a mediocre C+.

The Way-Back Machine, as I'm now calling it, goes dark.

Mr. O is silent.

"I hate her," I say. "That was really unfair. And seeing it after all these years hasn't changed a thing."

"I understand," Mr. O replies. "I've seen similar stories up here too many times to count, but I can give you a precise number, if you wish."

"That's not necessary."

"So what are you going to do?"

I shift around in my chair. "Can I have something to drink?"

"Coffee? Tea? Sarsaparilla?" Mr. O chuckles.

"Maybe something stronger?"

"Not until you're out of the Waiting Room. We have a wonderful selection of aged wines."

This information momentarily snaps me out of the unpleasant mood. "Really?"

"Absolutely. The best there is!"

I'm back in the somber mood. "How about some water?"

"Ice?"

"Yes, please."

An instant later the beautiful, handcrafted door—without a handle—opens up and a dog comes into the room, but it's not just any dog. It's *my* dog from when I was a boy!

"Timber?" I look from the dog to Mr. O in astonishment. "Is it really Timber?"

On Timber's back is a saddle-like contraption, and in the middle of the saddle is a pitcher of iced water with two glasses.

"I can't believe this," I mumble to myself.

Timber wags his tail and trots over to Mr. O.

All I can do is stare at what's going on with my mouth wide open.

"Thank you, Timber," Mr. O says, taking the tray and water from Timber's back. He gives the pooch an affectionate pat on the head.

Timber looks at me one last time with a puppy smile, tail wagging, and trots to the door. But before he leaves, I hear in my head, "You're doing good, Bob! Keep it up, and we'll be able to play with each other like we did so long ago!"

My eyes are wide open, my mouth agape. This can't be

happening! Before I can even mouth a response, Timber has trotted out of the room.

Mr. O states, matter-of-factly, "Things are much different here. And yes, that was Timber who spoke to you."

"How...how? I heard Timber—not that I've ever *heard* Timber before this, but...he spoke to me!"

"Like I said, everything is much different here."

"So Timber's in heaven?"

"Well, you saw him with your eyes and heard him speak to you, so yes, Timber's in heaven."

"But I'm in the Waiting Room, which is in heaven too?

"Let's move along here, shall we? Back to Mrs. Clavanese. You mentioned before Timber brought our refreshments that you hated her. Strong words, those. That's why the spoke is so dark. You've harbored that hate since that moment so long ago, and it had no place in you and certainly has no place here."

I fold my arms in front of me. "This is really unfair."

"Yes, it is unfair. Nevertheless, you know what you must do."

"What if I don't want to?" I say rather stubbornly.

"Well, there's always the Escape Tunnel, but I really don't think you're ready for that yet. Hopefully, never ready for that at all."

"This was so long ago, and I've forgotten about it...sort of."

Mr. O looks at me, direct and straight-faced. "Since the incident with Mrs. Clavanese, you've thought about it exactly 3,222 times."

"What? How can you possibly keep track of this?"

"Vee have our vays," Mr. O says in a fake German accent, reminiscent of Colonel Klink from *Hogan's Heroes*.

This cracks me up. It's all really too much to take in. "3,000 times?" I repeat.

"3,223 now; you just thought of it again."

Shaking my head, I say, "I thought we were supposed to have free will?"

"You do have free will, but you can't harbor hate and walk around the streets of gold."

"There really are streets of gold? I thought that was just a way of saying how great heaven is supposed to be."

"I'll show you personally once we get the spokes on the wheel lit up. How does that sound?"

Unfolding my arms and leaning forward, I give in. "OK, but she was so unfair. She hurt me. It took several grades for the kids in the class to stop teasing me about it. At one point, some of them began to call me Da Vinci. Yes, I hate her."

"You're now at 3,224," he points out. "See how it festers and still—after all these years—has control over you? All you have to do is think of her, and your stomach flips, your face scowls, you stop breathing, and your eyes narrow. All the good in you vanishes, and you essentially side with the Fallen One."

"The Fallen One? Who's he?"

"Someone who hated from the beginning, and those who follow him learn to hate just like him," Mr. O says.

Slouching in my chair, I grumble, "I don't want to hate anybody."

"So light up the spoke. Forgive her. Bless her."

I don't like this one bit. But I have the feeling that if I don't do this, if I don't forgive her, I'll be sitting here for who knows how long. Yet the "blessing" has to be real, authentic—otherwise it's not going to light up the spoke. Besides, as Mr. O has stated, you can't fake it. "It" knows when you're not 100 percent in.

Mr. O interrupts the silence and my thoughts. "Think of it this way. The forgiveness and blessing you bestow on Mrs. Clavanese, and everyone else we'll discuss, actually do two things. Yes, you are blessing the person, but that blessing frees *you* up in ways that are incomprehensible. Simply put, it unburdens you."

"OK. I get it. I know a weight was lifted off me when I forgave Ms. La Farge. I'm ready. I'll do it."

"Good!" Mr. O smiles and leans forward expectantly.

I take a deep breath and close my eyes, as it seems to help for some reason. "I bless and forgive Mrs. Clavanese. I…I…I bless her."

I'm almost afraid to open my eyes, but I do and look hesitantly at the wheel.

"Good form, Jack!" Mr. O cries out, satisfied.

"From *Hook*? Really? How do you find time to watch movies here?" I look at the wheel, and sure enough, the spoke that was all dark is now lit up. I follow the spoke to the end of it, expecting to see Mrs. Clavanese's picture, but there's nothing at the end of the spoke. She's not there. Confused, I ask, "Where is she?"

"Good question, but she made other choices in her life, so she's not here. She chose another direction—a dark direction. I can give you details, but it's better that I don't. Mrs. Clavanese was a very troubled woman who manipulated people all her life. She died bitter and alone. So sad. She didn't need to, but she isolated herself. That was the choice she made."

"So there's no hope for her now?"

Mr. O sadly shakes his head, signaling a definitive no.

Noting the seriousness, I ask again, "There's nothing you can do?"

"There's much I could have done, but Mrs. Clavanese had to ask. She never asked, so she never received. Simple, yet so elusive."

I look at the wheel, and there are still many dark spokes. I realize I have my work cut out for me.

As if reading my mind, Mr. O says, "Shall we do another?"

"Yes. I'm all in."

# 5
# FORGIVING GEORGE

MR. O ACTIVATES the Way-Back Machine.

I see myself and another boy walking quickly along a wooded path. It's just getting dark. I know where I am, and I'm around ten years old. I'm with my so-called friend George, the instigator behind the mischief I unwittingly find myself taking part in. He's two years older than I am, and as a ten-year-old, I'm entranced by the fact that I'm hanging out with one of the older boys. We are lugging a lawnmower motor we've stolen from a neighbor's garage. We're going to make a go-cart with the motor we've taken.

"OK, I had forgotten about this," I say out loud.

"Yes, but look at the spoke. If you go to the end, you'll see George's face."

I look where Mr. O is pointing. There he is, George, the older kid who got me in a lot of trouble. "George was a rat! He stuck me with the blame for stealing the engines."

"So there's more than one?" Mr. O peers at me over his glasses.

A quick beat of silence. "Yes, but some of them were all George's doing."

"But you broke into a neighbor's house and stole the engine, right?"

"Yes, but George was the snitch! He turned me in."

"George also taught you how to curse."

I pause for a moment, trying to remember.

Mr. O does something, and the Way-Back Machine changes images. I see George's father drinking at night. It's late, and the man is letting out a steady stream of obscenities. George is watching from the other side of the table, and he's laughing. His dad is actually teaching George to curse—to use the F-bomb and other four-letter words. George is all in.

The scene shifts. George and I are in his tree fort, and George is teaching me how to curse.

Next thing I know, I'm parroting George and dropping F-bombs all over the place.

"I forgot about this," I say with a more serious tone.

"You're forgiven for all this, but it remains part of your entanglement with George. Do you have any idea how many F-bombs you dropped throughout your lifetime?

"I'm not sure I want to know."

"87,622."

"That's a lot of F-bombs," I admit.

"Yes, it certainly is, but that's not the central issue. It's about George and your unforgiveness toward him."

"You mean I get a pass on all the F-bombs?"

"Yes, that's correct; those are covered."

"Covered?"

"When you accepted Jesus as your Savior, everything you have ever done that doesn't measure up to our standards here is *covered*—they're under the blood."

"I'm not sure I understand this."

"Well, it's mystical, supernatural, and in some ways beyond human understanding, but when Jesus gave His life on the cross… By the way, I know you know some of this, having had

Pastor Fred as your friend for all these years, so I'll cut to the chase. His blood paid for all the nastiness that human beings do—past, present, and future. *Behold the Lamb of God who takes away the sins of the world.*

"So the F-bombs, as horrible as they were, are covered. But not the unforgiveness. That lies with you and you alone. Only you can forgive or hold on to unforgiveness until it turns into a toxic root of bitterness. That's what we're dealing with here."

Frowning, I ask, "So the F-bombs don't matter?"

"Well, they do matter. But they're covered, like I said. However, the unforgiveness is something that lies within you, which is why we're in the Waiting Room. Only you can choose to forgive. Remember what the Good Book says."

"The Bible?"

"Is there any other book that's better? If you forgive those who have hurt you or sinned against you, you are forgiven. But if you refuse to forgive them, then you will not be forgiven."

"Which is why I'm in the Waiting Room."

"Very astute of you. Let's get back to George."

"He ratted me to the police when they went to his house."

"So?"

"He got off scot-free, while I got busted and was grounded for months. Not only that, but I also had to clean the bathrooms at our church for six months as a penalty. George and I parted ways after that. Later on, just four years later, he stole a car, got in a head-on collision, and died. Hard to believe; he was only sixteen years old."

"Well, that's not exactly what happened."

"That's what I was told. I remember reading about it in the paper."

"It's partially true. He did die in a horrible car accident, but he didn't steal the car. He bought it from his friend. He was running away. Do you know about his father?"

"That he was a drunk?"

"Yes, and he used to beat George—regularly. This is why George was running away."

"I didn't know about that. George never said anything about it."

"The summer before he died, George went to camp and met a counselor who befriended him there. George had never met anyone who showed love and acceptance toward him. Remember, his mother had left his father when George was a small boy. George's only role model was his abusive, alcoholic father. George was there for only two weeks, but it changed his life. The counselor told him the good news, and George accepted Jesus. George cried his eyes out when that happened, and for the first time in his life, he felt love.

"When he got home, he told his father, but his father exploded in rage and beat him until George passed out. His father beat him constantly, trying to get George to renounce his newfound faith and love for Jesus. That's why George ran away. Once he got his driver's license, he bought his friend's car. He had a plan and saved his money, but he never registered the car and kept it at his friend's house for fear of his father. So he didn't steal the car.

"His father found his Bible hidden in his room. When George came home from school, his father burned it in the fireplace; he spat whiskey on it, which fanned the flames as it burned. George had had enough, and that night he packed his clothes in a duffel bag. The next morning, when he got up, he acted like he was going to school. His father was passed out in the living room, so he never saw George leave.

"George went to school, but after school, he went over to his friend's house, threw his duffel bag in the back seat of his car, and left. He had no idea where he was going—only that he would put as much distance between himself and his father as he could. The first night, he slept in the back seat of this car. He was hungry and alone, but he was free. More importantly, he could pray and be with Jesus. The next day, while he was traveling on a two-lane highway, a tractor-trailer coming in the opposite direction blew out a front tire and careened head-on into George's car. George never knew what hit him. And you know what?"

"What?"

"He was escorted by a group of angels to his new home."

"So he's here?"

Mr. O nods and smiles. "No more beatings—ever."

"I heard his father died shortly after that."

Mr. O nods gravely. "Yes, he took his own life…sort of. He drank himself to death, and his liver failed."

"He didn't make it…here?" I ask.

"Some people never have a chance, and George's father was one of them."

"What do you mean he never had a chance?"

"His father was almost as abusive as he was. But what tipped him over the edge was when he fought in the Korean War. He saw things that, frankly, no person should ever see. He couldn't shake the memories, and they were with him every minute of every day and then at night in his dreams. There are some things people never recover from. This is what drove him to the bottle."

"I had no idea," I say.

"This is how sin is passed down from one generation to another."

"So where does the blame fall?"

"That's just it. How far back do you have to go before there is no sin? Where does the blame fall? In essence, you have to go back to Adam and Eve and the garden."

"I always thought that was just a myth," I say.

Mr. O shakes his head. "It's not. It's when Adam and Eve sided with the Fallen One, the Dragon, the Shining One. When they did that, they changed. Everything dark entered the human race. Death entered the human race. It was the ultimate game changer, and the Dragon thought he had won.

But actually, it enabled the protocols of the heavenly war; it set in motion the war that has been raging for millennia—and will soon come to an end. A time is coming on earth when there will be *no flesh, no sin, no death, no sting, and all because of the King*!"

"The King?"

"Yes, the King, Jesus, will return and establish His millennial kingdom on earth for a thousand years. Those who will return with Him on flying white horses will rule and reign with Him."

My head is spinning. "I don't understand…"

"Perhaps later I'll explain in more detail, but let's get back to George and his father. The newspaper article you read was only partially correct."

"I didn't know."

"This brings us full circle. So what about lighting up George's spoke?"

"By all means. I'm ready."

"Just to recap, this isn't about dropping F-bombs or stealing engines to make a go-cart. It's about forgiveness. Forgiving even when we don't see the whole picture…like with George and his father and his father's father, and back we go. As you, like everyone, forgive in the Waiting Room, you are forgiven."

I bow my head and struggle not to weep at what I've just heard—at what Mr. O has just revealed to me—and at what George endured without me knowing about it.

"I bless George. I pronounce blessings and goodwill to him. I forgive him."

I glance over at the spoke and watch as a ray of light shoots out from the center and lights up George's picture. To my astonishment, George's picture is there, but now he's waving at me!

"How is this happening?" I ask. "Is that really him? Is he waving at me?"

Mr. O smiles. "Yes, he is. He's happy to see you again."

"Hi, George!" I yell as I move closer to his picture.

"You'll see him at some point. You have a lot to catch up on."

"Another spoke to light up?"

"Yes, but before we get to that, I want to show you something in the Way-Back Machine that I think you'll really enjoy."

"What is it?"

"Just take another sip of your water while I look at your file, and then we'll see."

# 6
# THE FLAMING SWORD

YOU'VE BEEN DOING really well, and I'm proud of you," Mr. O says, smiling.

"Thanks, but in some ways it's a relief to get all this cleared up—to get the spokes lit up."

I look over at the large wheel hovering above the floor. Most of the spokes are lit up, but then again, some are not.

"You know, you did something when you were twelve years old that was really incredible."

"Is this going to be another dark-spoke-forgiveness thing?"

"As I said, you've been doing really well, so why don't we take a break and look at an incident from way back in your past. You know what? For the most part, you've forgotten about it."

"I have no idea what you're talking about."

"Well, let's take a look, shall we?"

Mr. O waves his hand over the Way-Back Machine, and the screen lights up.

Fascinated, I look closer. "How did you do that? How does this thing work?"

"It's complicated, but the short answer is that it's linked up to my thought waves, and I can communicate with it directly."

"Isn't this technology—super technology?"

"I bet you thought there was no technology up here." Mr. O chuckles.

"Well, yes."

"Just angels playing harps on clouds? Some people think that. I can assure you that is not the case. This place is the essence of creative thinking. Let me tell you a quick story. I'll put the Way-Back on pause for a minute."

The Way-Back's picture freezes.

Mr. O continues, "Do you remember the story of Adam and Eve?"

"Sort of."

"Here's the long and short of it. They side with the Dragon and are expelled from the garden, and then two cherubs are placed at the entrance of the East Gate."

"OK, but what is a cherub, and remind me who the Dragon is again?"

"Let's tackle the Dragon first. You might be more familiar with him by his common name, Satan. He was a liar from the beginning and a murderer. There is no truth in him at all. He's a deceiver, and it was he who led Adam and Eve down the path of darkness."

"OK, I think. I had no idea."

"Now, the cherub, on the other hand, is a very large, powerful, angelic being not to be messed with. Think *Dirty Harry*, only much larger."

"Dirty Harry?"

"I'm giving you an illustration so you can relate."

"But Dirty Harry?"

"Well, how about *the Lone Ranger*?"

"He was one of my heroes! How did you know?"

He laughs and motions with his arms for emphasis. "Mr. O knows all, sees all…"

I shake my head, grinning.

Mr. O pats the file next to him on the table. "It's all there.

Back to *Dirty Ha*…I mean, *the Lone Ranger.* So two Lone Ranger-type guards are placed by the East Gate to keep Adam and Eve from reentering."

"What about the other gates? Aren't they guarded?"

"Let's just focus on the East Gate for the moment. The two Lone Rangers are at the East Gate… Maybe we should make it the Lone Ranger and his trusted companion, Tonto. That's a better visual."

"Tonto was great! And the two of them together were my heroes."

"OK, OK, so the Lone Ranger and Tonto are guarding the East Gate. But guess what's between them?"

I'm reaching for an answer and shout, "Silver the horse?"

"Seriously?" Mr. O chuckles. "That's a good one. However"—he lowers his voice to create mystery—"it's something much more mysterious."

"What is it?"

"A flaming sword that turns every way."

"A flaming sword?"

"That turns every way. So what do you think this is?"

"I have no idea," I answer, captivated.

Mr. O holds his hands in front of him like he's holding a sword, and he pretends to wield it to the left and right. While doing this, he makes a sound, "Vroom…vroom…"

"Hey, wait a minute. That sounds like a lightsaber from *Star Wars*!"

"Where do you think they got the idea?"

"What?!"

"What do you think a *flaming sword is that turns every way?* Remember, Moses is writing this from his perspective."

"*The* Moses?"

"Yes, but don't get sidetracked. I know you weren't in Sunday school, so you missed a lot. But back to the flaming sword that turns every way. What do you think it is? Remember, Moses is writing this thousands of years ago. All he knows is firelight and oil lamps and a sword, which is a weapon—that's what he is familiar with."

"Seriously? You can go back that far?"

"Bob, time is irrelevant here."

Mr. O waves his hand over the Way-Back Machine, and to my astonishment the scene shows a lush garden with an entrance framed by a beautiful gate. At either side are what I imagine must be the cherubim—certainly a far cry from the Lone Ranger and Tonto. I am mesmerized by the scene. The angels are huge, foreboding—dare I say *holy*? A blinding light radiates from each one. There, in between the two cherubs, is what can only be the flaming sword. No one is wielding it, and it is turning every which way by itself. There's no way anyone is getting past that.

I'm stammering. "So it's real—all of it is real?"

"More real than you are."

Mr. O makes the lightsaber noise again. "Vroom…vroom…vroom!"

I laugh out loud.

"Well, let's get back to where we were, shall we?" Mr. O says with a sigh. He waves his hand, and the Way-Back Machine shows a beautiful summer day.

I recognize the place immediately. "That's Camp Arrow, the Boy Scout camp!"

"Yes, it is. Now watch."

It's a summer day, and I see myself walking along a path in the woods. I'm surrounded by a lush green canopy overhead. I'm by myself. Something small and furry is slowly walking down the path toward me.

"I can't believe it! That's my pet raccoon! That's Rascal the Raccoon!"

The raccoon is limping. He's alone and hurt. I watch myself go over to him and gently pick him up.

"It's OK, little guy. Are you all right? Where's your mama?"

I watch myself, a twelve-year-old Boy Scout holding the raccoon. The little furball curls up and buries his head in my chest.

I see myself turn around and hurry back up the path. Then the scene changes, and I'm in the nature lodge, and we're feeding Rascal milk with an eyedropper. He's hungry, and we can't get enough milk into him.

The counselor who is helping me with Rascal is about four years older than me. He's telling me what I need to do to help the little guy. We leave the nature lodge and head back to my tent. I have a couple of milk cartons as well as a syringe to feed him with.

The scene shifts, and I see myself lying in my single cot in the tent issued to me as a junior counselor.

Two other boys are in this hideaway of three tents about fifty yards from the main path. It's on a remote trail that no one would think of going down.

The little guy is curled up next to me on my pillow, and he's fast asleep. I'm petting him and just staring at him in awe and excitement because I realize I have a pet raccoon.

The scene shifts again. It's morning, and Rascal wakes me up by playing with my hair using his tiny front paws.

The scene shifts again, and I'm feeding Rascal some milk. I ask him tenderly, "How's your leg, little guy? Is it feeling better today?"

I see myself getting ready for the day as I dress in my Boy Scout uniform.

"Let's get going, Rascal." I pick him up and place him carefully on my shoulder. He acclimates to it as if he's been doing this forever, and even with his injured leg, his front paws are holding on to my shirt. His head is tucked underneath my chin. We hike up the path and head to the mess hall for breakfast.

I see myself enter the mess hall, and I'm surrounded

immediately by other boys shouting excitedly and pointing to my little friend sitting on my shoulder.

"Wow! Where did you get him?" a chorus of boys shouts.

I tell them how I found the injured raccoon.

We're at a table, and I get some fresh milk from one of the pitchers and make a little bowl of cornflakes and milk for Rascal. He devours it, taking the bowl in his paws and turning it every way to make sure he gets the last drop.

I'm smiling at the warm memory. "This is amazing. I had almost forgotten about Rascal. I kept him all summer long, but in the end I let him go back into the wild because his leg was better, and he was getting bigger. The nature counselor told me it was the best thing to do, so I let him go."

"Yes, but you helped him. And if it hadn't been for you, he wouldn't have made it. You did the right thing. Good for you!"

"He was my pet raccoon for the whole summer. He was such a great little guy. We slept together every night and went everywhere together during the day."

"You saved him, all right." Mr. O gestures to the wheel, and I see a spoke that's all lit up. There at the end is a picture of Rascal, but he's surrounded by other raccoons.

"He's got a family?"

"Yes, he did have a family. All because of you," Mr. O says.

"Can I see him again, like Timber?"

"Well, yes and no to that. It's a bit complicated, but yes, you can see him. But like Timber? Not quite yet."

"Can he talk like Timber?"

"All the animals talk here," Mr. O explains. "It makes for some very interesting conversations. Most of them have a great sense of humor."

"Wow." I'm nearly speechless.

"They love to laugh, and they laugh often. If two or three raccoons get together up here, there's no telling what will transpire, as mischief abounds!"

"Seriously?"

"Trust me, you have no idea what they're capable of. Some are on a probation of sorts." Mr. O chuckles.

"He was such a great pet." I reminisce. "I sure wish I could've had him longer than one summer."

"Well, as I said, you'll get to see him up here, although he's quite a bit larger than the last time you saw him. But you did the right thing in letting him go. All this also shows me your heart. You have a soft spot, and that's the most important thing."

I stare at the wheel, thinking of Rascal, and wonder what's next on Mr. O's agenda.

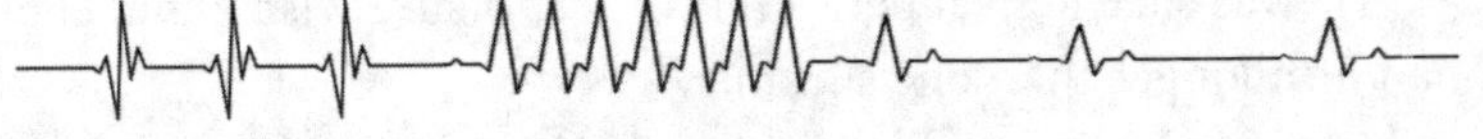

# 7
# GRACE FOR A BULLY

I GLANCE OVER AT the glowing wheel and wonder how long all this will take.

"That all depends on how fast you can light up the dark spokes," Mr. O replies.

"You're reading my mind again, aren't you?"

He laughs. "Of course. You're an open book. Hey, Bob," he says, excitedly, "watch me pull a rabbit out of my hat!"

Before I can say or do anything, a hat appears in his hands, and then with a mischievous smile, he pulls out a rabbit.

"Ta-da!"

"Rocky and…"

"*Bullwinkle.*" Mr. O finishes my sentence as we both laugh. "Laughter is good. It's the currency up here, if you get my drift. It makes the heart glad."

The rabbit is hopping around on the table as I'm cracking up at Mr. O's antics.

"OK, back in the hat with you." He picks up the rabbit, places it back in the hat, and then claps his hands together. Both the rabbit and the hat disappear.

"How did you do that?"

"Don't worry, it's not the first time I've done this. People who come here who are around your age appreciate it because most of them watched the cartoon show growing up. It's a way to keep the mood light, no pun intended, before we launch into another dark spoke."

Mr. O holds out his arms in front of him and wiggles his fingers as if he's getting ready to do another magic trick.

"So let's talk about the bullying you endured in seventh grade."

I nod my head and take a breath. "I've pushed that so far back that I almost forgot about it, but not really."

"You were in seventh grade, and the bully was in ninth grade. That's quite a difference."

"He had a mustache!" I exclaimed. "He would come up behind me when I was putting my books away and slam me into the locker. Then he would grab my arm and yank it behind my back."

"That's Karl, all right," Mr. O acknowledges.

"You know his name?"

"Of course. It's all right here," he says, patting the file. "Take a look at his spoke." Mr. O touches the wheel and somehow makes it revolve. Finding what he's looking for, he says, "Here it is. Take a look."

I follow Mr. O's finger, and at the end of the dark spoke, I see Karl's face from the seventh grade, snarling at me.

"Yep, that's the big doughhead. That's what I used to call him, the big doughhead. What a jerk."

"You've held a grudge all these years."

Sensing a turn, I begin to defend myself. "Yes, but…"

"No buts! You know how this works."

"Yes, but…"

"No ifs, ands, or buts!" Mr. O lets out a belly laugh. Birds of many colors—I think they're parrots—suddenly appear out of nowhere and start flying around the room. They're buzzing my head, and then one lands on my shoulder.

The parrot squawks while tilting its head: "You know how this works! How it works…it works."

"I can't believe this is happening. Yes, I know how it works, but…"

"Oops, there's that pesky word again!" Mr. O says.

The parrots fly away to a corner of the room and perch in a tree that has also suddenly appeared out of nowhere.

"Let's take a look in the Way-Back Machine and see what happens to Karl, shall we?"

The image on the screen springs to life, and I see Karl walking toward the boys' bathroom. His head is down, and he looks frightened. He opens the door and goes in, and four boys are waiting for him.

"You're on time this morning," one of the boys snarls with a sinister grin. Before Karl can do anything, they surround him and start punching him in the stomach and back. One of the boys takes Karl's arm and yanks it behind him. Karl yells.

"Are we hurting the baby boy?" another one of the boys taunts, hitting Karl in the solar plexus. Karl collapses in a heap on the floor.

The boys laugh, and one of them kicks Karl on his way out of the restroom. Karl is gasping for breath and moaning. A minute passes, and then Karl slowly gets up and makes his way out of the boys' room.

"This happened every morning that year," Mr. O says. "This is why Karl, the doughhead, attacked you. You see how the sin, the hate, the evil, the violence spreads? Let's look at what's waiting for Karl when he gets home."

Mr. O waves his hand. I see the doughhead walking toward his house. He opens the door, and there's his older brother waiting for him. He's much bigger and older than Karl. The Way-Back pauses.

Mr. O explains, "That's Tom, Karl's older and stronger brother. Watch what happens."

The playback starts again. As Karl enters the house and sees his brother, he turns instantly and bolts back out of the house, sprinting down the gravel driveway. Tom is faster and stronger, so he catches him easily, tackling and pinning him on the ground. He sits on Karl's back and presses his face into the gravel.

"I can't...breathe... I can't breathe..."

Tom slaps his brother's head on both sides, alternating with his left and right hands.

"I...can't...breathe..."

"What? I can't hear you?" Tom mocks.

"I can't...*breathe...*"

Then Tom reaches underneath Karl, grabs his crotch, and squeezes it. Karl yells out in pain and is writhing on the ground, but Tom is merciless and continues to hurt his brother.

Finally, he gets up and kicks him one last time before making his way back into the house, leaving his brother crying on the driveway.

The Way-Back screen goes dark.

Dumbfounded, I quietly say, "I had no idea."

"You see the way evil and hurt spread out like a cancer? There's no end to it. That's why the doughhead, as you like to call him, does the things he does. Karl's brother beats him—and abuses him sexually, but there's no need to show you that—and then Karl gets beat up in the boys' room every morning. Finally, Karl smashes you into the locker. It never ends; it's a ripple effect."

I'm stunned at what I'm hearing.

Again, one of the parrots flies over and lands on my shoulder, squawking, "Time to forgive...forgive." Then it flies back to the tree and joins the other birds, who make up a very noisy chorus repeating, "Time to forgive! Time to forgive!"

"That's really loud," I say, pressing my hands over my ears. When I look back at the parrots, the tree, along with the squawking birds, all vanish.

"What happened to the parrots?" I ask.

"I think they made their point," Mr. O replies, "so I returned them to their natural habitat, tree and all."

"Now I see the way violence spreads. Karl didn't have a chance, did he?"

"And I only showed you a portion of it. Do you know what happened to Karl? Well, Tom was six years older than Karl, so he got drafted and went to Vietnam. He was captured by the Viet Cong and tortured to death. They hung his body on a tree, along with other soldiers, and did some unspeakable things to them. They desecrated the bodies. When Karl heard about his brother's torture and death, he sank into a deep depression. He almost took his own life. He came very close to doing the unthinkable."

"What saved him?" I ask, soberly.

"He met a girl who was a Christian, and she told him about Jesus. Karl was head over heels for her. He told her everything that had happened to him: the sexual abuse by his older brother, the beatings he endured, the way he treated you and others. He confessed everything, and he wept bitterly. Anna told Karl that despite all this, there was forgiveness if Karl would ask. Karl ran across the finish line, as it were. They married later, and Karl went on to be a missionary with Anna."

My eyebrows shoot up. "A missionary? You've got to be kidding. Doughhead, a missionary? I don't believe it."

"Do you want to have a sneak peek?" Mr. O waves his hand, the Way-Back lights up, and there's Karl in some faraway land I don't recognize.

"Where is this?"

"Peru. And that's Anna, his wife. They run a food bank way up in the Andes mountains to feed the poor. Anna is a nurse, so they have a clinic too. They both speak Spanish fluently, and they hold church services. They've transformed the entire village in the years they've been there."

"This is incredible. Doughhead…a *missionary*?" I can't wrap my head around this. "That's impossible!"

Mr. O clears his throat and peers over his glasses at me. "All things are possible with God."

"Yes, but Doughhead a missionary?" I shake my head in disbelief.

"Well, what are you going to do? Should I bring the parrots back?" He chuckles.

"No, you don't have to do that. I'm ready…I think. Seriously, though…Doughhead, a missionary? Huh."

"You see, Bob, as I said earlier, human beings are in some ways like garbage dumps. Karl's life was more than a train wreck, yet he turned it around with some help from above—or I should say from here? Remember the story about two men who presented themselves at the temple? It's in the Good Book. One was rich and proud and patted himself on the back. The other was poor in spirit and knew he was a sinner. Who do you think scored more points?"

"I know the story. The poor man."

"Right, you are. He was poor in spirit, and that's what counts. Karl was poor in spirit, and he had no way out of his dilemma, yet he was healed, thanks in part to Anna leading him to Jesus."

"Wow, I had no idea."

"So do you forgive Doughhead?" Mr. O asks, grinning.

"Of course I do. Good grief. This is more complicated than I thought it was going to be."

"Everyone has a story—everyone. Actually, Bob, your story is not so different from lots of other folks who find themselves in the Waiting Room. There's good, and there's bad. And as I told you, most everything is covered. Everything but unforgiveness. That's why we're dealing with Doughhead, as you like to call him."

"I promise I'll never use that name again."

"You know what to do."

"Yes, I choose to bless Karl in every way possible. Is he still in Peru?"

"Yes, that video I showed you on the Way-Back was very recent."

"I had no idea. I haven't seen him in years, and he never went to any of the high school reunions."

"He was too busy helping others!" Mr. O laughs.

"Bless Karl. I forgive him. And I ask for forgiveness for harboring anger and unforgiveness toward him."

I turn toward the wheel to find Karl's scowl transformed. He's smiling and looks as happy and fulfilled as a human being can be. The spoke is all lit up and is, in fact, pulsating.

"Another spoke is lit up!" I say.

"Yes, but there's a spoke that, when we get to it, may be harder than you think."

"I think I know which one you're talking about."

"We'll get to it in just a bit, but first let's do something a mite easier."

And with that Mr. O waves his hand over the Way-Back, and I see myself in a soccer uniform.

# 8
# SINGING TREES AND PIPE ORGANS

MR. O IS paging through my file. "Aha! This is what I was looking for!"

"I can only imagine," I mutter.

"That's one of your favorite expressions, isn't it? It's also a really great song—one of my favorites."

Suddenly the chorus of the song "I Can Only Imagine" is playing in the Waiting Room.

"How do you…never mind. This place is really different, isn't it? Do you have radios up here? Is there a hidden speaker somewhere?"

Mr. O laughs. "Sound waves travel. And besides, where do you think music comes from in the first place? Have you not read in the Good Book that when the Lord appeared to Adam and Eve, they would hear His sound?"

"No, I don't remember reading that."

"Well, in the cool of the evening, Adam and Eve heard the sound of the Lord walking in the garden. Let me put it this way. Do you remember Jesus' triumphal entry into Jerusalem?"

"Isn't that Palm Sunday?"

"Yes, which in some ways takes away from what is really happening: Jesus fulfilling—to the minute—prophecies written hundreds of years before His entry. But I digress. Jesus tells the crowd that even the stones would cry out, and I can assure you that this is literal."

"Yeah, I've heard that in church, but isn't it just hyperbole? I don't think we can take that literally, right? Stones crying out?"

Mr. O raises his eyebrows. "It's 100 percent literal; the stones would have cried out. But let's get back to the sound in the garden. As the Lord is walking in the cool of the evening, the trees and flowers are singing to Him. That's what Adam and Eve are hearing. Here's the chorus again!"

The sound is somehow pumped up, and I hear the lyrics to "I Can Only Imagine." The last line echoes around the room and then slowly fades away.

I shake my head. "I don't see how that's possible, but I'll take your word for it."

"All things are possible with those who love the Lord. Here, let me show you."

Mr. O claps his hands together, and suddenly we're standing in a redwood forest. Shafts of sunlight are piercing the thick canopy overhead. A gentle wind blows the subtle scents of the forest toward us, and then I hear it—music. Music like I've never heard before.

"Where are—"

"Shhh! Just listen," Mr. O whispers with excitement.

Complex melodies fill the air along with others that are simple; they are playing over and around each other, yet somehow are all in harmony.

"Here come the redwoods!"

I hear deep bass notes, which rumble throughout the forest floor, causing the ground to tremble.

Through a shining smile, Mr. O says, "All creation worships!"

The music swells to a flawless crescendo, and then silence—and I feel a wave of perfect peace wash over me.

In a flash we are back in the Waiting Room.

"How is it possible to go there and back again in the blink of an eye?" I ask, amazed.

"I could tell you, but it's too complex for most people. Even Albert had trouble with it."

"Albert?"

"Oh, sorry," he says. "Einstein. Albert Einstein. Can I play you one of my favorite pieces of music?"

"What about Einstein? Wait, you have a favorite piece of music?"

"I have lots of favorites, but this one piece is just amazing! Have you heard of Johann Sebastian Bach?"

"Yes, but I've never really listened to much of his music."

Suddenly I hear the sound of a *huge* pipe organ.

Mr. O's excitement is contagious. "Listen to when the bass pedals are pushed!"

The entire room is vibrating—as if we're experiencing an earthquake—as I hear a *very* low bass note that shakes the walls of the Waiting Room.

"Wow!" I blurt out.

"That's an understatement!" Mr. O is enthralled. "This was Bach's 'Toccata and Fugue in D minor.' Listen to where he takes it…incredible! Talent on loan."

"Hey, that's a Rush—"

"…Limbaugh quote. Where do you think he got it from?" Mr. O laughs. "Shhh, here it comes." He holds his hands out in stillness, waiting for the moment.

I listen intently as a cascading stream of notes and melody reverberates around the room. I'm afraid to move a muscle; the music is so captivating.

"A far cry from what is pawned off as music nowadays," I quip.

"True, but each has its place. Although I call Bach the father of Western music. He's so unappreciated now, and most of your young people have no idea who he is. Let me pump up the volume here."

The music continues to shake the walls. Its thunderous low pedal notes seem to vibrate my rib cage. The complex melodies cross over each other in perfect harmony.

I mutter, "I had no idea what I was missing."

Mr. O and I listen, enraptured, to the rest of the piece. At the end Mr. O stands and applauds, motioning me to join him. I rise from my seat and clap enthusiastically.

"Good ol' Johann was and still is amazing. He holds a concert here every fortnight. The venue is packed—standing room only!" He laughs heartily.

"Every fortnight?" I repeat, flabbergasted.

"Yes, standing room only. But let's get back to your file. Take a look."

Mr. O waves his hand over the Way-Back, and I see myself playing goalie in a soccer match.

"No! Not this! I can't believe you're showing me this!"

"Shhh. Watch."

I see myself running out from the goal toward a player who is bearing down on me. There is no player from my team to defend me from this guy, who looks like he's flunked a few grades—he's huge. I run out to meet him as he kicks the ball toward me. I see myself dive heroically at the ball. I cover the ball with my body, and the guy kicks me in my side as he goes for the ball. The referee blows his whistle, and a penalty is called.

"Nice defense," Mr. O says.

"Thanks. The idiot of a coach, Mr. B, never gave me any kneepads or other protective gear. He never let us drink water, so we were always dehydrated. He made a big deal of *not* giving us water," I spewed. "What an idiot. He was a big, loudmouthed, idiot of a coach."

Mr. O stares at me, eyebrows skyward. "Really?"

"Yeah, and he would make us do these laps around the soccer field. I played for one year, hated every minute of it, and never tried out for soccer again. You know what? I can't watch a soccer match on TV to this day. It affected me that much."

His eyes are still on me. "I know."

I continue my rant, saying, "Then there's the shot that went right through my legs. I never lived it down."

"You mean this one, right?" Mr. O shows the replay, and there I am, as the soccer ball is kicked right between my legs.

"Yep, that's the one." I groan.

I watch as the opposing team is laughing, pointing, jumping up and down in delight, almost in disbelief that I have let a goal go right through my legs.

"You weren't paying attention, were you?"

"Nope. I was somewhere else."

I watch Mr. B call a time-out and then yank me out of the game. My teammates are shocked. The assistant coach is shocked, and frankly I'm shocked that I let the ball go through my legs.

"On the bench, Frisbee, and no water!" Mr. B yells. He gets in my face in front of the other boys.

"How could you let that happen? What were you thinking? Or does that pea brain inside your skull think at all? You have the attention span of a gnat!"

I hang my head in shame.

"Marshall, get out there and be goalie!" Mr. B yells. "Frisbee, hit the locker room. You're finished playing on this team."

I see myself slowly get off the bench and make my way to the locker room. The screen goes dark.

"We lost by one point, and that's the goal I let through my legs. I really never lived it down. I hated Mr. B the rest of high school. When we had our ten-year reunion, I got even. By then I was an airline pilot, so when Mr. B came up to me and tried to humiliate me, I shot him down. What a jerk."

"There's his spoke. It's very dark."

"It should be. Even after all these years, I hate him."

"*Hate* is a strong word."

"Maybe so, but I hate him. Jerk."

"So you want to carry around the hate? It's festering in you like a rotten apple. I'll remind you of this. What happens if you run into 'the jerk' up here?"

"Mr. B, the jerk, is here? No way!" I bristle at the thought.

"You'd be surprised who's here and who isn't. Yes, Mr. B is here."

"What if I go out of my way to avoid him? Is that possible?"

"To a point. But sooner or later you'll run into him, although he looks much different from the Mr. B you knew in high school. And he's not limping anymore."

"I can't do it," I say.

"Yes, you can. Look how far you've come. Light up his spoke. Forgive him."

I fold my arms over my chest, incompliant. "I'm not going to do it."

Mr. O takes his glasses off. I can tell he's serious now. Leaning forward, he says, "Do you really want to have the weight of your unforgiveness hold you back? Keep you in the Waiting Room… waiting? Unforgiveness weighs you down."

"I don't feel weighed down. I feel vindicated."

"Remember, it's not about him. I agree that Mr. B acted like…a jerk. But think of it this way. How did Mr. B become a first-class jerk, to use your vernacular? Do you want to see?"

"No." I feel my stomach tighten.

Mr. O waves his hand, and then the playback resumes. "There is Mr. B as a young boy."

I look only with a side glance, but I can see Mr. B is limping and has braces on his legs. "What's wrong with him?"

"He's got polio. Now watch."

I'm watching closely. I see Mr. B, the crippled boy, playing catch with a man I assume to be his father. The man is yelling at him, saying, "Stop throwing the ball like a girl!" As the ball is thrown back to him, the boy misses the catch, and while trying to get it, he falls to the ground.

His father shakes his head and walks away.

Then I see Mr. B, the boy, start to cry. His mother comes out and comforts him, but I can tell that the damage is done.

My tone is different now. "That explains why he walked with a slight limp years later when he was our coach."

"You see the way events shape our lives," Mr. O imparts, "the way a careless word or action can have a ripple effect and change someone's life for better or worse?"

I nod silently and look away.

"Trust me, you'll feel better, and lighter, if you forgive him."

"I hate to admit it, but you always change the equation by what you show me on the Way-Back."

"That's why the Waiting Room is so important. You can get all the facts, which, in most instances, change the condition of the heart," he says. "Always lean to the side of grace and mercy. Always."

"OK," I concede. "I know how this works. I forgive Mr. B, and I bless him. I'm sorry for the way I harbored anger and… hatred toward him all these years."

"Look, it's lighting up!" Mr. O points to the wheel.

I look over, and sure enough the spoke is lighting up. There's Mr. B with a smile on his face—and he's waving at me!

Suddenly I'm floating upward. I float above the table, and now I'm up at the ceiling, which has to be at least twenty feet above the floor.

"Hey! What's going on?"

"I told you that you'd feel lighter," Mr. O says with a hearty laugh.

Then I hear what sounds like applause coming from outside the room.

Still floating, I ask, "What's that? People clapping?"

"Yes, that's your cheering section. You'll meet them when you're all through in the Waiting Room."

I feel myself slowly descending from the ceiling, and then I'm back in the chair. "People clapping? They can hear what's happening in here?"

"Yes, they have a ringside seat, as it were. Isn't it good to feel lighter?"

"Yeah, I have to admit it is. I do feel like a weight has been lifted off me."

"It has, my son. It has."

# 9
# THE REFUSAL

LOOK AT THIS." Mr. O points to the Way-Back Machine.

I recognize the scene immediately. "Nope. Uh-uh. No, I'm not going there. I don't want to see this."

"I don't blame you," he said, soberly. "This is a hard one. And if you look at the spokes, this spoke is one of the darkest. There's no forgiveness here; there's only a lingering, festering…dare I call it, cesspool of hatred and loathing? A deadly combination."

I put my head on the table and mumble, "I know."

Mr. O folds his hands in front of him, leans in toward me, and says, gently, "Can I tell you something?"

"I don't have a choice in any of this, do I?"

"Of course you do. There's always the Escape Tunnel. But as I have hinted to you, the Escape Tunnel is a last resort. I don't think you really want to go there."

"What's so bad about it?"

"It's not a very comfortable place to be, I can assure you of that. Let me tell you something about people."

I pick up my head and stare wearily at Mr. O. "Fire away."

"With some people, but not everyone, the unforgiveness becomes toxic." Mr. O pauses to let that sink in.

"Toxic?"

"Yes, toxic. Unforgiveness can lead to bitterness, and if left unchecked, it can cause major health problems such as ulcers, heart disease, and even cancers."

"You're being serious?"

"Oh yes, 110 percent so. Bitterness, unchecked, never leaves. Unforgiveness festers. Hate can consume a person. Do you remember your Aunt Mary?"

"Yes. She was really beautiful as a young woman, and a devout churchgoer who never missed a Sunday. But something happened to her, and she became...*twisted* is the word that comes to mind."

"She died a very bitter woman who refused to forgive those who hurt her, including her husband, who physically abused her. I spent a lot of time with her here—in the Waiting Room—but she never changed. Nothing I could do would help her. It is, as you know, free will. She opted for the Escape Tunnel and never returned."

"What happened to her?"

"Well," he says, "let's not talk about that for the present. Do you remember what she died of?"

"Some sort of cancer, I think, but I'm not sure."

"Yes, cancer of the stomach, and then it spread into her intestines. Yet she would never let go of the bitterness. Here's something for you to think about. Bitterness and unforgiveness are also gateways to the dark side."

"The dark side...like Darth Vader?" I laugh, but I can see Mr. O is very serious. "Sorry."

"The dark side is all too real and is still manifesting in the disobedient sons of men, even as we speak. Bitterness is a door, an open invitation for unclean spirits to take up residence in a person, and then things go downhill from there."

"So Aunt Mary was demon-possessed?"

"No, not possessed, but certainly oppressed in many ways. There is a difference between the two. She listened to their voices, always blaming and accusing. Eventually the cancer manifested."

"Are you saying that sickness is…"

"Caused by our thoughts and unforgiveness? Yes and no. It can certainly create a very unhealthy countenance in a person, age them quickly, and lead to sickness. But not in all cases."

"I still don't want to look at the Way-Back."

"I don't blame you. But you *need* to look, because when you do, it will eventually set you free."

Mr. O gestures to the Way-Back, and it lights up. I see my first real girlfriend, Michelle. She's with her best friend, Paula, and they are walking on the side of the road. I know all too well what is about to happen, but I force myself to look. It's nighttime and late, past midnight. What were they doing out there that late in the first place? Then a speeding car strikes Michelle from behind. As she is flung into the air, her head snaps back against the windshield, breaking her neck.

"She never knew what hit her," I get out, just as a wave bursts from deep in my core, sending burning tears down my face.

Mr. O nods.

"She was my first real girlfriend. When we first met at the YMCA, I was sixteen, and she was fourteen. We were together until she got killed. I was eighteen then, and she was sixteen. It was young love—puppy love—but it was real. We would talk for hours about everything. Her death changed my life."

"Yes," he points out, softly, "and eventually you accepted the Lord because of what happened."

"Yes, but that was years later with my best friend, Fred. He was my roommate in college. Why was she taken? Why was she killed? Where is she now?"

"I could tell you, but we have to deal with the person who was driving the car first."

"I know her name, but I never met her. And you're right…I never forgave her…and I still don't! She hid from everyone for years, and then it came out five years or so after the hit-and-run that she had been the driver. I read about it in the local paper that Paula mailed to me. I couldn't believe it."

"And that's why you're here." Mr. O gestures toward the wheel as it rotates. Then it comes to a stop. Through my tears I see a very dark spoke—it's all black.

"This is really bad," Mr. O says, nodding toward the dark spoke.

"I don't care how black it is." My words are smeared with tears. "I'm not going to forgive her. We never found out who did the hit-and-run until five years after Michelle was lying in the cold, dark ground…at sixteen years old! Her life was snuffed out in an instant! Paula said that Michelle's body rolled off the hood about one hundred yards from where she was initially struck. It was too dark, and she didn't get a good look at the license plate. Michelle's parents were heartbroken, and so was I. It took me years to process it. And even now, when I think about it, I get angry."

"Festering, isn't it?"

"Yes, but I'm not going to light up that spoke. Can't we just take this one out of the wheel?"

Mr. O slowly shakes his head. "Remember what I told you about all actions being covered?"

I nod my head and feel sick to my stomach.

He continues, "Everything is covered except unforgiveness—that rests solely on you."

"I can't do it," I say, shaking my head. "I can't! It's not fair!"

"Are you really saying you can't or that you don't want to?"

"Both."

"Is that your final answer? Are you sure?"

Folding my arms, I declare, "I'm sure. This girl essentially murdered Michelle and then most likely drove off to a nice, cushy life somewhere, leaving everyone devastated. It took me years to get over it, and in some ways it comes up to haunt me even here."

"The choice is yours. It is free will. Are you sure you can't forgive this person who killed Michelle?"

"I'm sure," I say, unmoved.

"I'll ask one last time. Look at the wheel and all the people you've forgiven since you've been in the Waiting Room. You can do this too. You can forgive."

"Nope. Not gonna happen. There are some things you don't come back from and some people who don't deserve forgiveness."

"Really? Remember when Jesus was hanging on the cross? He was whipped within an inch of His life. His hands and feet were nailed to the cross, the thorns digging into His scalp. What did He say? '*Father, forgive them, for they do not know what they are doing.*'"[1]

"I get it"—I'm twisting in the chair with grief—"but that's Jesus, and I'm not Him. I can't possibly forgive the person who killed her."

"Remember, Jesus is fully God and fully man. He forgave, saying, 'Forgive them, for they know not what they do.'"

"Nope."

"There's always the Escape Tunnel, so you can escape from all this and hold on to your unforgiveness."

I nod. "I guess that's for me then."

"Are you sure?"

"Yep." My hand taps the table in emphasis. "I'm sure. This is a line in the sand for me, and I won't cross it. End of story."

"I'm really sorry to hear this. If you want to go and escape and be alone with your bitterness and unforgiveness, that's your choice, and I won't stop you from making it. However, if, while you're in the tunnel, you find that you don't like it there and want to come out, just forgive and we'll come and get you."

*What have I gotten myself into here?* "Come and get me? What's so horrible about the Escape Tunnel? Why would I have to call you to come and get me? Who's coming to get me?"

Mr. O continues without acknowledging my questions. "Remember, though, only if you forgive her will we come and get you."

"I'll say it again, that's *not* going to happen. I can't!"

"Well then, follow me." Mr. O sighs as he pushes his chair back and motions for me to follow him.

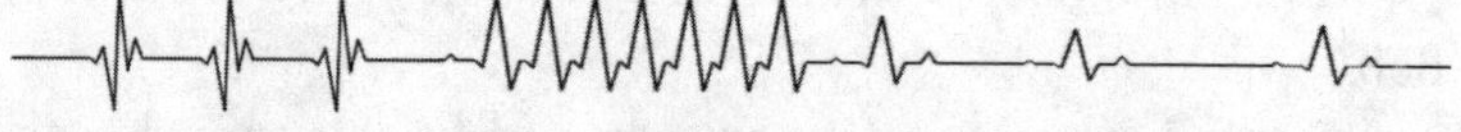

# 10
# THE ESCAPE TUNNEL

Suddenly one of the walls opens up, and there before me I see a tunnel. It's dimly lit but looks inviting. I can hear soft music coming from deep inside. Its walls are smooth, and its ceiling is at least ten feet above the steps that lead down. I can see platforms about every twenty feet, and positioned next to them are lights, which are in niches in the tunnel wall, casting their soft light on the path.

"This looks inviting," I say as I scan the territory.

Mr. O doesn't say a word. He just motions for me to go into the tunnel. I take a few steps into the tunnel and then *shhooop*—there's a sound behind me as the entrance suddenly closes, and I don't get a last look at Mr. O.

I start descending the steps and reach the first platform, where I pause and look at the lights in the niches. Then something weird happens: The light coming from where the door to the Waiting Room was goes out. I look behind me, and the entrance where I was less than a minute ago seems wrapped up in darkness. I continue down the steps. Suddenly a beautiful young woman is running toward me.

"Bob! Bob? Is that you?"

In an instant she's standing in front of me.

"Aunt Mary?" I ask, hesitantly. "Aunt Mary, is that you?"

She laughs and strokes her shoulder-length blonde hair with one hand, fixing it in place.

"Yes…Aunt Mary! After all these years, it's good to see you, Bob."

"It's good to see you too, but where does this tunnel lead? Why are you so young?"

"One thing at a time, Bob, but follow me down."

"Down…where?"

"Come on, Bob. Follow me down."

Mary starts down the stairs. Once she reaches the next platform, she turns and motions to me to follow her. I take a few steps off the platform I'm on and start down to her. When I reach her, I notice that the platform where I first met her is now dark; that light, too, has gone out.

"Where are we? What is this? I'm not escaping like I thought I would. I'm not sure I like this."

"You've only just arrived, so give it some time, Bob. Here, take my hand, and we'll walk together."

I take Aunt Mary's hand, and my hand recoils instantly—her hand is ice cold. There is no warmth in it at all. Nothing but cold. It's almost like holding the hand of a corpse.

"Why is your hand so cold? Where are we going?" I ask again.

Suddenly I feel something claw at my back. I quickly spin around, but there's nothing—no one—there.

I shout, "Something sharp just clawed my back!"

"Really?" Mary laughs. "I wonder what could possibly do that here?"

I look around, and as I do so, I see Mary's face. Just for an instant, all the flesh has shrunk into her skull. Her skin has a greenish hue to it, and her teeth are sharp and dagger-like. I turn around and start to make my way back up to the landing we just came from, but I find that somehow I can't go there. Something is holding me back.

"You can only go down, Bob." With that she grabs my hand and *forces* me down a flight of stairs to the next landing; I am amazed by her strength. Then I hear laughter, and it's coming from below us, but it's not good laughter. There is no merriment in it; there's only mocking…and it's coming closer.

"What was that?" I'm getting nervous.

Before I can say anything else, I feel another sharp, claw-like object tear down the length of my back, and I cry out in pain. Again, I turn around instantly, but this time, to my shock, I see a grotesque human shape, a skeleton with skin that seems to be falling off it. Its hands are claw-like, and it claws at the air between us and then snarls at me, baring its fang-like teeth.

With a start I instinctively step back.

"What's wrong, Bob?" Mary laughs, but it's a mocking laugh.

Before I can react, Mary claws at my face with her long, red-painted fingernails, and I feel blood trickling down my face.

"Wha…What are you doing?" I don't know what's happening, but I'm shocked that Mary would do something like this.

Before I can do anything else, another figure comes out of a cleft in the wall. The figure is hunched over, and its clothes are tattered. Whatever it is, its stench precedes it, and I am gagging at the smell.

"Bob, so nice of you to join us!" Before I can react, the hunchback punches me in the solar plexus, and down to the cold floor of the tunnel I go.

Mary drops to her knees, and her face is pressed against mine as she laughs mockingly. "Are you escaping, Bob?" She claws at me again, and I cover my face with my hands, but I feel her nails dig deep into the skin on the back of my hands. Then the skeletal figure that was behind me claws at my legs, and I scream. I am in a state of raw terror. I feel the hunchback kick me. All three of these ghouls—because I think that's what they are—are hurting me nonstop.

The hunchback bites my ear, and I feel his teeth sink into my flesh. Between his clenched teeth and in a deafening wail, he screams, "Welcome to outer darkness!" And with that he bites down and takes a piece of my ear off. Mary claws at me again. Her face is horrible to look at. Gone is the young girl; in its place is a nightmarish figure with green skin and yellow eyes.

Another kick from the hunchback.

"Yes! Outer darkness!" Mary yells as she claws at my eyes. I try to cover them, striving in vain to protect myself. All the light suddenly goes out. I hear in the distance other voices who are screaming—yelling obscene things, horrible things, and nightmarish, dark, sick, and perverted things. The sounds of them echo through the Escape Tunnel, and I realize there is no escape here. They are all around me. The stench is unbearable, and there are too many of these shadow figures to count. I feel my legs and arms being held by different ghouls, and I am being pulled apart.

"Draw and quarter him!" someone yells. And with that my limbs are stretched to their limits, and I am screaming from a pain I have never felt in my life. A hand smashes into my genitals, and I writhe in agony.

"Draw and quarter him," another voice squeals in evil rapture.

"Outer darkness!" I recognize Mary's voice cackling.

The torture has become unbearable; I feel I may lose consciousness. For an instant I wonder how this can be happening. I died and was in the Waiting Room, but now everything has changed.

As the ghouls are pulling as hard as they can on my limbs, I realize they will shortly come out of their sockets. A thought enters my mind amidst my agony.

"Forgive her."

I know it's Mr. O. He's somehow reached me here in what I now identify to be outer darkness.

I realize I'm not escaping from my unforgiveness; I am in a living horror show. I scream out in pain. They keep pulling on my limbs. I hear something snap, and I realize my shoulder has been dislocated. My foot is being twisted, and I feel my ankle snap.

"Outer darkness!" Mary yells at the top of her lungs, her nails digging into the other side of my face.

From deep within my soul, like a bursting geyser, I cry out with everything in me, "I forgive her!"

Suddenly, a blinding light erupts in the darkness. The ghouls scream as they run back down to where they came from. The hunchback is running toward his crevice in the tunnel wall.

"No! No! No! Don't do that!" Mary screams. Her hands ball up into fists, and she is about to hit me.

The light becomes brighter. The ghouls cover their faces as they run down the tunnel, trying to escape the white radiance. As I am released from their grip, I collapse into a heap on the floor.

Then I feel a strong arm come under me and lift me up. I'm being held by someone. I can barely open my eyes. The light is so blinding that I can't make out a face, but I think it must be an angel. He's holding me to his chest, and we're ascending out of the tunnel, out of outer darkness. I feel myself being set down. I'm back in the Waiting Room, except I'm on the floor, huddled. A blanket of light envelops me, comforts me, heals me. I can feel my limbs being put back in their normal positions. The pain has left, and a warmth that is centered in my solar plexus spreads to all parts of my body. I am somehow being supernaturally healed of the wounds inflicted on me.

I sit up slowly and stretch out my arms, realizing I'm all here; nothing is broken. My wounds have been healed. My legs are fine. My face is fine. I look over at the table, but Mr. O isn't there. The door appears, and he walks in.

"Glad you're back! I see your wounds are healed," he says, adjusting his glasses on his nose.

"Did that really just happen? Was that my Aunt Mary? Who are those…ghouls?"

"*Ghouls* is an appropriate word for them. They are the undead. They have chosen not to forgive, and they claw and bite and kick and punch each other and anyone who is unlucky enough to venture there for the first time. It's their choice to remain there. All they need to do is forgive, but they choose not to. I'm glad you're back here. Take your seat. Would you like something to drink? Maybe a snack?"

"I've just come back from…hell…and you're offering me a snack? Seriously? Who was that who rescued me? Was it an angel?"

Mr. O ignores my questions. "How about some nice hummus and chips? I know that's your favorite snack." Mr. O pats the file next to him. "You called out and forgave, and you were rescued."

"Well, who rescued me? Who was it? How did he know where to find me?"

"What kind of chips? Pita?"

"All my wounds were healed, and here I am. How is this possible?"

The door behind Mr. O opens, and in comes—I can't believe it—my grandmother. Except she looks like the picture I saw of her sitting on the beach when she was a young woman.

"Hi, Bobby. So nice to see you again." Smiling broadly, she's holding a beautiful silver tray. On it are the hummus and pita chips.

I'm overwhelmed—no, stupefied would be more accurate. I don't even know what to say. Grandma comes over to my side of the table, sets the tray down, and then lovingly pinches my cheek.

"You're doing really well, Bobby, so keep it up and know that you're in really good hands with"—she winks at me—"with Mr. O." She leaves the room but not before waving one last time to me. As the door closes behind her, I see a burst of light from where Grandma was standing.

"Was that really my grandma?"

"Yes, it was."

"How does she look so young?"

"She's in what we call her *glorified body*. She got an upgrade." Mr. O chuckles.

"What happened to Aunt Mary? When she first appeared, she looked young too, but then she turned into a horrible hag with green skin hanging off her face." I shudder at the recollection.

"Well, as I told you, your aunt will not forgive, as is the case with everyone in the Escape Tunnel, which really is what I call *outer darkness*. The door is always open to her, and I've seen people who have been there for a long time finally come to their senses and forgive, and then they are freed. Essentially, each person there has the key to their own self-induced prison. Their final destination is in their own hands. If they forgive, they are released."

I shudder again as I recall what happened just a short time ago, yet now it seems like a distant memory from the past.

Mr. O continues, "Now that you have forgiven, let me tell you something. Michelle was taken from you, and that was life-changing for you. But the girl who was driving the car was so traumatized by the accident—seeing Michelle dead on the hood of her speeding car and then rolling off onto the road—that she blocked out the entire event from her mind. She never stopped to see whether Michelle was alive because she was deeply traumatized. She repressed all memories of it until one night years later. She awakened, and the memory surfaced. She became hysterical and sank into a deep depression. She did drugs for several years until she finally forgave herself. She also tried to find you, but you had moved away and were in college. She was heartbroken and dedicated her life to helping others. She became a counselor. She specialized in restoring and healing people with PTSD and suppressed trauma, just like she experienced."

"That does change the equation," I say with a new openness. "It's like once the whole story is told, it changes everything."

"I'm glad you forgave. We can now move on to other spokes on the wheel. Look." Mr. O points to the wheel, and I see the very dark spoke light up! I hear the sound of applause coming from outside the Waiting Room.

"I hear the applause again. Is that for me?"

Mr. O's face lights up with joy. "Yes, it is. The applause is just for you."

"Well, who are the people out there who're clapping for me? I can't believe this..."

"You'll see them once you finish lighting up all the spokes."

I start lifting off the chair again. "Hey! I'm going up to the ceiling again!"

"Feeling a bit lighter, are you?"

"I do. I do feel better, lighter, happier."

"And you're one spoke closer to lighting up your wheel!"

I slowly descend back down to my chair. "So what's next? How do you keep track of all this? Do you do it with everybody? This is making my head spin."

"Only with those people who have unforgiveness in their hearts. By the way, this is almost a full-time job for me—and I never get a day off."

"So what happens now? How many more of these spokes do I have to light up? And when they all get lit up, then what happens?"

Mr. O glances at the wheel. "You still have work to do, but you're doing well and proceeding at a good rate. You'll have your wheel lit up in no time."

"What's the next spoke on the wheel?"

"Like I said, this one should be fairly easy for you, yet in the end the choice is yours. It is free will."

"You keep reminding me of the free will part, but how can this be free will if I can't remain in my unforgiveness? That's not really free will, is it?"

"Like I said, what happens if you run into the woman who killed Michelle up here and you have bitterness in your heart? Then what? We can't have people in glorified bodies who hate each other here. Think of it this way. Long ago, a group of angels here decided to take matters into their own hands. The results of this, the Rebellion, are still echoing through the ages and have created havoc on earth. However, a time is coming soon when this will stop. It's coming soon."

"What's coming soon?"

Mr. O pushes his glasses up on his nose and leans forward, looking at me. "The second coming of Jesus. In fact, His white horse has been getting anxious, prancing about, leaping into the air, flying around in a big circle, and then landing again. I think the horse knows something that a lot of people up here would love to know."

"Wait a minute. Are you saying that Jesus' horse can…fly?"

"Yes, fly, and so can the armies of heaven that accompany Him on His long-awaited return. Have you never heard this? '*I saw heaven standing open and there before me was a white horse, whose rider is called Faithful and True….His eyes are like blazing fire, and on his head are many crowns. He has a name written on him that no one knows but himself. He is dressed in a robe dipped in blood, and his name is the Word of God.*'[1] Here's one of the best parts. Are you ready?"

Captivated, I nod and lean forward.

Mr. O continues, "'*The armies of heaven were following him, riding on white horses and dressed in fine linen, white and clean.*'[2] So let's walk through it. Jesus is on His white horse, and so are the armies of heaven. However, the last time I checked, there was no dusty trail for the armies of heaven to get to earth. Will Rogers will attest to this!"

"Wait...Will Rogers? Here?"

"Oh, yes. He's been giving riding lessons here."

"Come on! You've got to be kidding."

"Well, a lot of folks up here have never ridden a horse. Will does a really great job."

"So what happens?"

"As I said, there is no trail-o'-dust that leads from here to earth, so how do you think the Lord's army gets to earth?"

"I don't know. I've never thought about it."

"And that's the problem. Most of you listen to what's in the Good Book but never think about what's written literally. You never think about things like what I just pointed out. Think about it. How do the armies of heaven arrive on the earth? They have to fly. And here's one more gem for you. Those riders on the horses, the armies of heaven that accompany Him, do you know what happens when they all land in Jerusalem?"

I shake my head. "I don't have a clue."

"Well, those horses are Father's gift to all those in that army. They're called the *White Horse Police Force*."

"Police Force? White Horse Police Force?"

"Think about it. When the Lord returns, there are maybe four billion people who have no idea what's going on. This is where the White Horse Police Force comes into play. Everyone is on a flying white horse, and this army—His army—is dispatched to all points on the earth. Those riders rule the cities that the King has put them in charge of. They preach the good news, heal the sick, and raise the dead. Welcome to the thousand-year millennial kingdom! Where Jesus rules from Jerusalem."

I ponder what I just heard. "A literal thousand years? Really?"

Mr. O sets his hands on the table, and there appears the Good Book, as he calls it. "Read this for yourself." He turns the pages, and after finding what he's looking for, he turns the Book around so I can read it.

I look at the page and realize I can't understand a word. "What is this—Greek?"

Mr. O laughs. "Sorry." He waves his hand over the book, and the text language changes to English. He points to a verse. "Read here. Read it out loud."

I do as he asks. "'Coming out of His mouth is a sharp sword....He will rule them with an iron scepter.'"[3] I look up at Mr. O. "So this is literal? Jesus rules from...Jerusalem?"

"Well, it's certainly not Walla Walla, Washington!" Mr. O cracks up. "Those who have ridden with Him from the heavenly realm will rule with Him. Everything changes. No more wars. No more dishonesty. No more prostitution. No more stealing, lying, or killing. It all changes, and those who are part of the White Horse Police Force will enforce this. In short, no more lawlessness."

"It just seems like a fairy tale. I mean, everything you just said has been going on from the beginning with no end in sight. So He's really going to rule from Jerusalem?"

"Trust me. He will, and it may be sooner than you think. Remember, what was written will come to pass; what was foretold is unfolding."

I let this sink in. It's a lot to process, and I'm not sure I can. "I'll have to think about all this. But since I'm here, I won't get to see any of it, right?"

"Why don't we go to the next spoke on the wheel?"

Once again Mr. O has avoided my query. With that he gently turns the wheel and points to another dark spoke. But I am somewhat relieved, as it's not nearly as dark as the one that sent me into the Escape Tunnel. I shudder at the thought of that terrifying experience, and a cold chill runs down my spine. I'm getting this. Forgiveness is the key that unlocks everything. Forgiveness is what I will do from this point forward.

# 11
# THE COSMIC WAR

Mr. O is looking at the wheel intently. There are fewer and fewer dark spokes, and the other spokes are brighter and seem to be coming "alive." Mr. O turns the wheel and gestures to yet another dark spoke.

"Well, Bob, what do we have here?"

I lean forward and follow the dark line to the end. As with all the spokes, there is a picture of someone I recognize easily—it's my father. He looks sad, broken, defeated, out of sorts.

"That's my dad as a young man. He had just gotten back from the war and was shell-shocked and broken. He never got any help."

"Is that you he's holding in his arms?"

I lean forward to get a better look at the infant.

"Yeah, that's me."

Mr. O goes to the Way-Back, and with a wave of his hand, the scene comes to life. I see my father holding me and rocking me gently. His face is sad, and there are dark circles under his eyes. Then a slight smile slowly eases its way through his pain as I voice my approval in baby babble at being rocked.

"We were never close. He never taught me anything except to

rush through whatever we were doing to get it done as quickly as possible. It took me years to undo that so-called work ethic. I learned to be attentive and absorbed, focused on my work to enjoy the process of whatever I was doing, and not to rush through it to get it done. What's that saying? 'Haste makes waste'? That was Dad—one, two, three, finished. I thought that was the way everyone worked."

"That's all he knew."

"Like I said, he never taught me anything about life, about women, about friendship, about how to be successful, about how to love a wife, or even about how to find a wife. I got nothing. Not even how to balance a checkbook! Nothing. Squat. He was detached from my life. He was never there."

Mr. O waves his hand over the Way-Back. "Well, that's not entirely true. Here's your dad at Boy Scout camp with you. He gave up a week's worth of work to be with you on that campout."

I nod my head, remembering. "Yes, he was there, but we never really connected…even there. We had nothing in common. Nothing."

"But he did love you and your brother. That much is true."

I look back at the picture of when he's holding me as an infant. "Why does he look so sad? So broken-down?"

"Do you want to see why?" Mr. O queries.

I stop and think for a moment, wondering whether I'm ready for this. As with everything here in the Waiting Room, I'm learning that there are always two sides to every story and people may not be who I have assumed them to be. I realize that my perception of people has been faulty. I think back on my neighbor, Ms. La Farge, who was abused by the Germans and, like many people who survived that event, never recovered from the abuse and horror inflicted on her as a young woman.

After thinking, I begin, "I know he went through hell in the war, but he never spoke about it. He kept it all inside him. I remember one time I asked him about it. I think I was thirteen years old or around that age. He started to talk about it, and then less than a minute later, he burst into tears and ran out of the room. My mother told me not to bring it up again, so I never did. I've always wondered what happened. I know that whatever happened, it kept him from being the man he could have been. It always hung over him like a shroud of darkness. I remember one night he woke me up when he was yelling loudly. I heard my mom trying to wake him up. He was having a nightmare. Then he started to cry. I could hear his sobs from the other room. I didn't know what to do."

"You're right," Mr. O says somberly, "your dad was a broken man. Some people never heal from events that happen in their lives, like Ms. La Farge and your dad."

"It seems so unfair. But they didn't do anything to deserve the things that happened to them—the horrible things that changed their lives forever."

"I know; it's not fair. But remember the kingdom of darkness is still at large and rules the affairs of men on earth…for a time. Although, that time is coming to an end soon."

"How soon? How 'bout next Wednesday!" I sigh.

"All I can say is soon."

"In the meantime, people suffer, like my dad—and pretty much everyone we've talked about since I've been here."

"There will come a time when the entire earth will change and be made new. Every tear will be wiped away, and men and women will no longer remember the former things. Healing will come to the nations."[1]

"But in the meantime, the brokenness, the shattered lives—like my dad—remain as they are. It's not fair."

Mr. O pauses. "Think of it this way. Jesus is hanging on the cross. What has He done to deserve capital punishment, death? Nothing. He was broken for all mankind. '*Behold, the Lamb of God, who takes away the sin of the world!*' The cross is what the Dragon never considered. Nobody understood it. Not Mary

Magdalene or Mary, His mother. Not John the Beloved, His disciple. No one. Not even the Dragon."[2]

"I'm not sure I'm following you on this."

"How can you kill God? You can't kill God…or can you? No one imagined this—certainly not the Dragon. This is why the crowd that gathered around Jesus at the crucifixion is taunting Him, telling Him to come down from the cross. Make no mistake about it—He could have come down. This is what the two Marys who were there—His mother and the other who was a disciple—and John the Beloved were expecting. They knew He was God in the flesh. In other words, fully God and fully man. *No one* gets it—no one. However, Jesus, who is God, dies. His body becomes lifeless, and His soul and spirit depart, heading down to the lower parts of the earth where He proclaims to the spirits who are in prison that they're not getting out!"

I'm riveted at this thought. "There were spirits in prison?"

"Yes, those fallen angels who came to earth and married human women. It's complex. Look at it this way. Man is perfect when he's in the garden. Adam and Eve are innocent, and then the Dragon beguiles Eve, and the rest, as we know, is history. Yet in the scene that follows shortly after is the essence of what I call the *cosmic war*."

"Cosmic war?"

"The cosmic war is stated in this one sentence, which is the gateway to the rest of the Good Book: Your seed—your offspring—will be at war with the seed, the offspring of the woman. He, the Messiah, will crush your head, and you will bruise his heel."[3]

"I don't understand this. Whose offspring?"

"The offspring of the Dragon. Satan will be at war with the offspring of the woman. In other words, it's a seed war between the two, but I prefer to call it a cosmic war because that is what it really is."

"So Jesus dies? What does that have to do with the cosmic war?"

"Everything. Let me explain. Mankind is locked into an endless cycle of sin and death after the garden. Added to this is the influx of the Dragon's fallen angels, who are trying to corrupt the seed, the offspring of the woman. This is the reason for the flood of Noah."

"You mean with the animals and the boat and everything?"

"It's not just a story, as almost every culture around the globe has a flood story. The Dragon sent his troops to earth. They married human women and mixed their seed with them and created a soulless hybrid known as the Nephilim. This was the reason for the flood of Noah. It was judgment and resulted in wiping out the abomination of the Nephilim—at least for a time."

"So the story about Noah is true? I thought it was just a story to tell kids in Sunday school."

"I can assure you that it was real. It was really the first clash between the kingdom of light and the kingdom of darkness. Can you imagine if the bloodlines of humans were contaminated with fallen angel DNA? There would be no humans left! The Dragon would have won the cosmic war, and planet earth would have been his to rule over. But that's not what happened. Noah was pure in all his generations; his bloodline was not contaminated with the blood of fallen angels. It's a move and then a countermove throughout the Good Book.

"So getting back to the cross with Jesus. No one expected Jesus to actually die. As I stated, how can you kill God? Yet what seems impossible happens, and He dies on the cross. But here's the amazing part of the story. His blood and death pay for all the sins of the world from Adam to you," Mr. O says, pointing a finger at me.

"My...sins?"

"Everyone's little nasties, yours too, that people try to hide and pretend are not there: the lying, cheating, stealing, lustful thoughts, murder, wanting what others have, and jealousy. And on and on it goes."

I think for a minute on what Mr. O has just explained before I reply.

"I get it. The list you just read off seems to be the sad state of human affairs."

"Then you add the endless wars that have raged for centuries and continue to do so, even as we speak. Do you know what?"

I shake my head. "I don't have a clue."

"When He comes back—when Jesus returns to earth—there will be no more war. Think about it. No more human beings killing each other, no more genocide, no more butchering. It stops when His feet touch down on the Mount of Olives in Jerusalem. But let's get back to your father. As you know, his life was never the same after the war. He never really recovered from the nightmare he experienced. However, he's here now, and everything is different. There is only love and goodness here."

I'm almost speechless as the reality of the Waiting Room is sinking in. "Can I see him?"

He smiles. "Of course you can. Just as soon as we're done here."

The moment is very sobering. I find myself tearing up. I put my head on the table and weep. I feel Mr. O's hand on my shoulder, and a surge of warmth and peace courses through me.

"It's OK. You're doing fine…light up his spoke," he whispers.

My body is shaking from crying, but after Mr. O puts his hand on me, I feel a peace I've never felt before. I wipe the tears from my face and look at Mr. O. "I bless my father. I forgive him. I bless him."

With that the spoke on the wheel lights up, and suddenly the room goes dark, and fireworks appear overhead. It's the best fireworks finale I have ever witnessed. The ceiling has all but disappeared, and high overhead are golden bursts of red, blue, and brilliant white shapes.

"Wow! That's incredible!"

Mr. O is watching too. "Here's one of my favorites," he says, pointing overhead. A huge, brilliant starburst suddenly appears, and then clusters of light fall toward us, landing on the table, next to my chair, and all around us. These balls of light turn into rabbits that are running all around the room, to Mr. O's delight.

"OK, everyone, that's enough," he says.

A large hole opens up in the floor, and then the rabbits disappear into it. The fireworks stop, and the room slowly lights up again as before.

"Good work, Bob. Let's continue, shall we?"

# 12
# WHAT HAPPENED TO MARY?

"YOU'RE THINKING ABOUT your aunt, yes?" Mr. O is peering at me from behind his glasses. His hands are folded in front of him, and I can see by his expression that he's very serious.

"How did you know?"

"It's written all over your face. Here, take a look."

Mr. O somehow reaches below the table, produces a mirror from it, and passes it over to me.

"How did you…? Never mind."

I am somewhat hesitant to take it, but I do. I look at Mr. O, trying to get an idea of what he's up to, but he's not giving anything away. I hold up the mirror to my face and look.

"Oh my gosh!"

I literally have "What happened to Mary?" written all over my face in different-colored markers.

"This isn't permanent, is it?"

"Look again," he says, gesturing with his hand.

I glance at the mirror again, and all the writing is gone from my face.

I smile as I shake my head. "Well, that's a relief."

"True, but back to the matter at hand." He puts the mirror

back under the table. I lean down to see where the mirror has gone, but there's no drawer or shelf.

"Where did the mirror go?"

Mr. O chuckles. "Back where it belongs. A place for everything and everything in its place."

Leaning toward me, he says, "Let's get serious. You're wondering about your Aunt Mary. Why?"

"How long has she been down in the tunnel, in the outer darkness?"

"Too long. And I agree with what you're thinking—you should try to get her out of there."

"How did you know? Never mind." I mumble, "*Written all over my face...how ridiculous.*"

"So would you like to try to free her? To get Mary to forgive?" he asks. "As I told you, that's the key to her self-induced prison. If she forgives, she's free and restored and out of outer darkness."

Surprised at this, I ask, "Is there a way to free her? I want to help her, but I'm scared. No, that's the wrong word. I'm terrified of going back down there."

"I can help you with this," he states, plainly.

"Seriously?"

Mr. O cocks his head, and his eyes twinkle. I can see he's up to something, but I have no idea what.

"I can protect you if you want to go and see if you can help her. But first I have to tell you what Mary is holding on to, the incident that has bound her up in unforgiveness. When she was alive, it festered to the point where she died of stomach cancer, and she still wouldn't release it. As I told you, I spent a lot of time with her, but she wouldn't let it go. It is free will. No one is sent to outer darkness; they go there by their own free will." He pauses and looks at me intently. "Just like you did."

I shudder as I remember the Escape Tunnel.

"I'm not sure I want to know what happened."

"Well, that's a good place to start. However, if you want to help her, you need to know what happened to her."

I'm thinking about Mr. O's words. Part of me wants to know what happened to my aunt that traumatized her to the point where it took control of her life and, from what Mr. O stated, actually killed her.

Mr. O begins, "When Mary was young and had just married her husband—you never knew him because they divorced before you were born—Mary had a lifelong friend, Mildred. They did everything together all throughout their teenage years. They married their husbands on the same day in a dual ceremony. Then, after a while, they both became pregnant. Mary and Mildred would get together each day and measure each other's growing bellies. They were joined at the hip and ecstatic about raising the babies together."

"So what happened?"

"The time came to give birth, and their babies were born just a few days apart. Everything seemed good at first. But then Mary's baby had something wrong that the doctors couldn't explain, and after three days, the child died. Mary never recovered from that. She tried to conceive again but had three miscarriages. Mary's relationship with Mildred soured, and she never spoke with her again. Her husband divorced her a few years later and started a family with another woman. Mary grew bitter and hit the bottle to escape. She became an alcoholic. The Mary you knew put on a good front, but the reality was completely different."

"No one ever told me any of this."

"People often hide who they really are. They hide and put on a false front, a facade if you will, but inside they are tormented by what has happened to them."

"Who can blame her? She lost her child! That's not fair. What's the point of that? Why?"

"It's complicated, but I'll try to simplify it—not that it's simple at all. When Adam and Eve sided with the Dragon in the garden—when they fell for the lie—the deception *that they would be like God, knowing good from evil*, changed everything, and death entered the world. Death is the Dragon's calling card. He comes only to rob, steal, and destroy. The baby's death was the work of the Dragon. Do you want to know something?"[1]

I nod, not knowing where this is going, but I am unsettled.

"The baby is here. He's not a baby anymore, and he's... whole."

I shake my head, not knowing what to make of it.

"Everything evens out," he says. "'*All things work together for good*,' even when we don't see it. Sometimes the good happens on earth and humans can see it; sometimes it happens here, as in the case of Mary's baby."[2]

"Yes, but look at what happened to Aunt Mary," I protest. "Her life was ruined."

"While it is true that Mary's heart was broken at the loss of her baby, she could have done what King David did so long ago at the death of his baby boy. Do you know the story?"

I shake my head no.

"King David had a child with Bathsheba, who became David's wife through some very unscrupulous means. I won't go into the details, but when they came together and she became pregnant and gave birth, the child grew ill and died. David prayed and pleaded that the child would be spared, but he wasn't spared and succumbed to his illness. Here's the point. David had been fasting and praying that the child would recover, and when the child passed away, David stopped fasting and returned to his duties as king. His servants didn't understand; they thought the death of this child would have sent David into the abyss of mourning. David said something that has staggering implications. He stated this: *That he knew someday he would see the child again...when he passed from this life*. Indeed, that is exactly what happened."[3]

"Yes, but how does a person even deal with the pain, the loss, the torment that I assume goes on every day for the rest of their lives?"

Mr. O nods and lets out a deep sigh.

"Let's take a moment to review what we talked about before and add a little more to it, because it's important. You're right. The pain is overwhelming. Think of what Jesus' mother, Mary, must have felt. Remember, she knew He was fully God and fully man, and she was at the foot of the cross, most likely thinking, '*He has to come down soon.*' Because how can you kill God? You can't, can you? This is what Mary was thinking. But the reality was something no one—not even the Dragon himself—saw. Jesus is both fully God and fully man. '*In the beginning was the Word, and the Word was with God, and the Word was God.*'[4]

"Jesus is the Word made flesh—fully God and fully man. He died—the man-part died—and His body lay in the tomb for three days. But you can't kill God, right? That's what's so amazing. Jesus' spirit and His soul rejoined to His body, and He was raised from the dead. The firstborn of the dead. The prototype for the rest of humanity rising from the dead."

I shake my head, wondering what this has to do with Aunt Mary and the loss of her baby. I echo, "The prototype?"

"Think about this. If eternity is stretched out before you, like here, where there is no time as you knew it while you were on earth, and all things are reconciled, then all things work together for good. The Good Book says, '*Behold, I shew you a mystery; we shall not all sleep, but we shall all be changed, in a moment, in the twinkling of an eye, at the last trump: for the trumpet shall sound, and the dead shall be raised incorruptible, and we shall be changed. For this corruptible must put on incorruption, and this mortal must put on immortality.*'[5]

"That's the promise of the resurrection. He is the *firstborn from the dead. The prototype*! You can't kill God! The body is in the tomb for three days. This—Jesus rising from the dead—was unthinkable to the Dragon, and it was essentially *checkmate,* the end of the ongoing cosmic war. However, even though Jesus declared victory, He has not yet ascended to His throne. He has allowed the Dragon to continue his rule on earth…but only for a time."

"Why doesn't He come back and set everything right?"

"Yes, the whole creation groans," he says knowingly. "But I'll tell you a mystery. The protocols of this *heavenly war* are not revealed to the people on earth, so certain things are hidden from humans. Things that humans can never comprehend. Things that are best left where they are. But in the end, He will wipe away every tear. That's the promise. But back to your aunt."

Feeling at a loss, I ask, "What can I possibly do for her that you haven't tried already? I can't explain any of this the way you just did. What do I tell her?"

"You can tell her that you've seen her son."

With that Mr. O somehow starts up the Way-Back, and I see a man around thirty years old, in his prime. He smiles and waves at me. "Hi, Bob!"

Stammering, I ask, "He…he knows…who I am?"

"He's been waiting for this."

"Seriously?"

"Very seriously. Why don't you wave back?"

I wave hesitantly to Mary's baby who's not a baby anymore. "What's his name?"

"Do you see the white stone that's hanging around his neck? His name is written on it."

I peer into the Way-Back. "I see the stone, but I can't make out the writing. It's like something from *The Lord of the Rings.* What is this—Elvish?"

Suddenly Gandalf's hat appears on Mr. O's head.

Cracking up, I say, "That's hilarious!"

"Laughter is always good for the soul, but with some people

laughter is a thing of the past, like with Mary. There is a name on the stone, but it's written in the heavenly language, which is why you can't read it. For now, just wave, but you can tell Mary that her son is here and is whole, hale, and hearty."

The Gandalf wizard hat disappears, and he continues, "Everyone here has a white stone with their name written on it."

"Will I get one?"

"Yes, but you have to finish up here first, in the Waiting Room. However, I'm going to give you your white stone early because you'll need it when you go to help her. It will not have your name written on it...yet."

"How is that going to help me?"

Mr. O reaches into his pocket and produces a white stone necklace. The unusual stone is set in what looks like glowing gold, and it's attached to a silver chain. It's very beautiful.

"That's mine?"

"Yes, it is. And later it will have your real name on it." Mr. O gets up from the table and walks behind me. He places the white stone necklace on my chest and fastens the clasp of the silver chain behind my neck. "This will protect you."

I look at him.

He answers my silent question. "You'll see in just a minute when we enter the Escape Tunnel."

Just hearing the name sends a shiver down my spine. "Are you sure this will protect me?"

Mr. O raises his one eyebrow and gives me a look.

I think I recognize that look. "That's—"

"Spock, from *Star Trek*. Yes, I know. Very effective look, yes?"

With that I follow Mr. O to the Escape Tunnel, which looks like the other walls in the Waiting Room except for the flashing red neon sign that reads, "*Escape Tunnel.*"

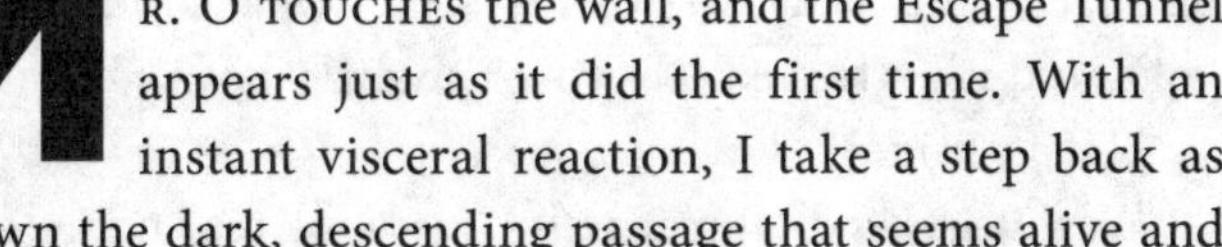

# 13
# BACK INTO THE TUNNEL

MR. O TOUCHES the wall, and the Escape Tunnel appears just as it did the first time. With an instant visceral reaction, I take a step back as I look down the dark, descending passage that seems alive and ominous. Mr. O moves closer to me.

"This will not be like the last time," he says. "Follow me a few steps into the tunnel."

I watch as Mr. O moves into the tunnel. The lights are dim, just like the last time, and I hear the wind in the distance. If this wind had a name, it would be *forlorn*.

"It's not like the last time, Bob. You have the stone. Come here, and I'll show you."

I really have no choice but to do what Mr. O is asking me, so I take a very tentative step into the tunnel to stand in front of him. He reaches out and touches the white stone that is hanging just above my chest and then slowly pulls his hand away. A light emanates from the stone; it's faint at first, but in a matter of seconds it has grown to a brilliant sphere that lights up the tunnel. Though it is very bright, the light doesn't hurt my eyes to look at. It has a warmth to it that I can feel, like being bundled in a warm ski jacket on a cold winter's day. I feel protected in a way I've never felt before.

Mr. O continues with his instructions. "This light will go with you, and the beings that are there will have no power over you in any way. You have the authority. You have dominion. You have my power, which is the light itself. So as you descend, you will watch the brokenness flee from before you. You will hear the sounds of torment, as these souls who are here, by their own choosing, hate the light. The ghouls, as you call them, will flee from it. They will shriek at it. '*The light shineth in the darkness; and the darkness comprehended it not*.' Yet if these ghouls would turn and forgive, they would be whole, joyous, and free from the burdens and the torment.[1]

"Go and find your Aunt Mary. The light will guide you. Follow it. When you find her, tell her about her son. Ask her to forgive what happened so long ago. Tell her that you forgave too, and that it is now *well with your soul*. Tell her that her forgiveness is the key to her prison."

I'm frozen, inundated with things I've never seen before. I wish there were some training manual, *How to Navigate the Terrifying Escape Tunnel* by Mr. O, but there isn't one. There are only the words and brief instructions from him.

"How will I find her?"

"The light will guide you. Call her name, and she will come to you because you have the Power of the White Stone. Even though she has chosen darkness, there is still some hope that she will respond to it. Are you ready?"

"Not really, but I sense I have little choice in the matter."

Mr. O smiles and gestures for me to move farther into the tunnel. I take my first step, and light is all around me. It gives me a confidence I have never experienced before. The light is dispelling the darkness! I take a few more steps and look behind me. Mr. O waves and motions for me to keep moving. Bolstered by the white stone and the light shining all around me, I wave back and start walking faster down into the darkness.

I can still hear the wind; it's louder now. And there are voices being carried by it—pitiful wailings and deep moaning from somewhere far below me. I press on. To my right I see a figure moving away from me as I draw closer to it. The person's clothes are nothing more than rags. For just a moment, we make eye contact as the ghoul turns its head to look at me. I can't tell whether it's a man or a woman, but the look is the personification of despair and hopelessness. I have seen homeless people many times. They have a look of despondency and detachment, almost like the walking dead, but this, here in this tunnel, is something far worse. It's almost impossible to call these ghouls human.

The figure lets out a desperate cry. Whipping its head around, it brings its hands to its face to shield its eyes from the light, and then it scurries back into the darkness. I stop for a moment and wonder what unforgiveness has caused this person to spend who knows how long in this darkness, in this hopelessness. I press on deeper into the darkness, yet the white stone has formed a wonderful bubble of light all around me. It is comforting, and the light is *shattering the darkness*!

I continue my descent. I can see that the steps end in the distance, and then a very broad platform stretches out in all directions for what seems like miles.

I take the last few steps and find myself standing on the dark platform. Its surface is rough, and I can feel the unevenness of it through the soles of my shoes. The wailing and desperate cries come from all directions. There is a smell here—no, perhaps *stench* is a better word. It reminds me of the time Timber, my dog, brought home the carcass of a dead raccoon. It had been decomposing for days, and the stench was unbearable. I had to give Timber three baths to get the smell out of her coat. That stench is here, and it is the same—the smell of death.

I'm wondering how I'll ever find Mary when the light begins to move to my right. I am still in the wonderful bubble of comfort, and I remember Mr. O's words, so I follow the light. The light is guiding me. I see ghouls everywhere scurrying away from me. Some are clawing at the light from a safe distance, as if trying to harm it, but to no avail. Others are screaming, shielding their eyes, and running in all directions. Some have collapsed on the ground and are weeping uncontrollably and gnashing their teeth.

The light grows brighter, which makes the ghouls only react louder and more intensely. Some are cursing; others are turning on their fellow ghouls and begin punching, hitting, and biting one another. Looking at this scene, I shudder and move to the center of the light.

The light once again begins to move, so I follow it. I don't want to be here, but seeing all this makes me determined to at least try to get Aunt Mary out of this place.

The light stops. I stop with it and look around. I know this is where I am to call out for Mary. I don't know how I know; I only know that she is here, nearby.

I raise my voice amidst the tumult. "Aunt Mary?"

Suddenly all is quiet. The ghouls have stopped their screeching, leaving only the forlorn sound of wind.

"Aunt Mary?" I call out again.

To my left I see someone coming toward me. I know it's her, but she's hunched over, broken, shattered, almost beyond recognition.

Mary lifts her head, and her eyes are wild-looking, like a cornered animal. She takes a step and then collapses to the ground, banging her head on it repeatedly.

She lets out a long wail of anguish.

"Aunt Mary! It's me, Bob! Don't be afraid. I've come to help you out of here. I know about your baby and all that happened. Mr. O told me. I saw your son—he's alive!"

"It's a lie! It's a lie!" she shrieks. "My baby is gone! He's gone."

"No, Mary, he's alive, and I saw him! He's there. You can see him too."

"He's gone! I hate God. I *hate* Him! Why would He let this happen? It's a lie…it's a lie!" She puts her head in her hands and wails.

"I know, Mary, but things have worked out here. Your son is alive, and he's whole, hale, and hearty! You can see him. I can help you see him!"

I see Mary's body heaving as she sobs. This goes on for a bit, and then she stops and picks her head up. She crawls toward me, closing the space that's between us.

"You saw him?" she growls. Her lower lip is quivering, and her hands, even though clasped together, are trembling.

"Yes, he's alive," I entreat. "I saw him with my own eyes. He's alive and a grown man. He's waiting for you."

Mary crawls closer and sits up about ten feet from the bubble of light. She's shielding her face, but she's looking right at me.

"How can that be?"

"Your baby is in eternity, and he's a grown man now. When he died so long ago, angels escorted him right to heaven. There's no time there, and everything is made right there. All tears are wiped away. All things are made whole. Everyone there is healed of everything. I know you had only three days with him, but now you have *eternity* before you…if only you will forgive."

Mary is nodding her head. I can see that she's thinking about all I just said. She's drooling and crying softly.

Finally, she says, "How…how do I…? What do I…do?"

I take a deep breath. "You only have to forgive everybody of everything. That's all. You can do it. Just forgive." She seems heartened by my words.

She collapses again, her hands hitting the ground in front of her, but there is no strength left in her. I can see she is letting go of all the bitterness. She turns her hands so that her palms are facing up. She is trembling all over; her body convulses in deep spasms.

"You're doing it," I whisper.

Then something incredible happens. The light emanating from the white stone around my neck begins to grow and slowly go toward Mary. She is still sobbing, but her hands are lifted slightly off the ground with her palms facing upward.

The light is creeping toward her, and then it surrounds her foot. Mary's arms fall to the ground, and she lies very still. There is no sound now. Even the wind has stopped its infernal howling.

I'm astonished at what I see next. Her body is being transformed from where the light has touched her as it spreads slowly upward. Her clothes are being changed too. I can see that everything is being made new! I look at her hands and watch as her claw-like fingers are being remade. They look young again—soft, supple. Her body convulses, and the light has surrounded her. Her sobbing continues, but everything is recast. She is clothed in white linen—white and clean and pure. And her hair, matted and disheveled before, has taken on the appearance of when she was young. I watch as it grows out in long, blonde strands. Her sobbing stops. She sits up and then turns to look at me. Her face is young, refashioned, and a smile spreads across it. She begins crying again, but these are tears of joy.

"Thank you…thank you, Bob. Thank you," she whispers over and over.

I'm crying too. I have just witnessed something I can barely grasp. Mary stands up and runs toward me. I open my arms, and she tumbles into them. We are both crying out loud now with joyful tears.

The light is moving, but I find that we are moving with it. It's almost as if we are sitting in a vehicle of some sort. We're standing, but the light is taking us back to the stairs I descended just a short while ago.

Faster now, we are racing up the staircase, and the ghouls are nowhere to be seen. We reach the top step and the door to the Waiting Room, and standing there smiling, with his arms outstretched, is Mr. O.

# 14
# THE REUNION

THE LIGHT BUBBLE begins to fade. Before it goes out, Aunt Mary, who is young and beautiful again, runs into the arms of Mr. O. She is weeping, and her face is buried in his chest. Mr. O holds her close, speaking softly to her. I can't make out what he is saying. He slowly takes a step back, almost like he's dancing with Mary into the Waiting Room. I follow. The light bubble that surrounded us is almost gone. I'm filled with wonder as to how all this works together. My fingers find the white stone hanging around my neck.

We are all safely in the Waiting Room, and the Escape Tunnel door has closed, leaving just the sign above its place on the wall of the Waiting Room. Suddenly there is music. I listen, transfixed—it is the most beautiful music I have ever heard.

"Well done, Bob!" Mr. O exclaims as he begins to dance with Mary. The joy on their faces lights up the room. Mr. O looks like a professional ballroom dancer. He's really light on his feet, and he's twirling Mary as she laughs with joy.

"Well done!" Mr. O exclaims again.

I'm not sure what to say, so I nod my head silently in agreement. I'm not even sure what just happened, and I'm running the whole thing over and over again in my mind. I do know that Mary was transformed right in front of me. I saw it! I was in the bubble of light as it raced up the staircase, transporting us safely from the outer darkness. Here we are—whole, hale, and hearty!

I watch as they continue to dance until the music comes to an end. Mr. O bows to Mary, who then curtsies in response, and they both laugh.

"Are you ready to see him?" Mr. O whispers to Mary.

Mary nods her head enthusiastically.

"He's on his way now."

Mary's face lights up like I've never seen it before. Her countenance radiates joy.

"I can't believe it," she says instinctively.

Mr. O. chuckles. "You will believe it soon enough! In the meantime, how about some refreshments?"

Instantly my file on the table is gone. In its place and out of nowhere, a punch bowl appears along with a silver tray with some artfully arranged and tasty-looking sandwiches on it.

Mr. O pulls a chair out for Mary and attends to the punch bowl, handing the first glass to Mary, then to me, and finally to himself. He raises his glass. "To the King!"

"To the King!" Mary repeats.

Mr. O looks at me, and I join in, even though I don't know who the King is. But I'm all in if Mr. O and Mary are, so I echo, "To the King!"

"Help yourself, Mary." Mr. O gestures toward the silver platter full of sandwiches.

"These are delicious! What are they?" she asks as she motions toward the delectable nosh.

"Some would call it manna from heaven, and, in fact, we have some of the finest chefs that have ever walked the earth up here. You can't believe some of the concoctions they come up with," Mr. O exclaims.

I take a bite. "These *are* really good!" I realize I've never tasted anything so wonderful.

Mr. O bows, smiling wide. "I'll make sure I tell the chefs."

I grab another of the tasty treats and stuff it into my mouth, relishing the novel flavors.

"It appears your taste buds are doing backflips," Mr. O discerns as I munch away.

I look over at Mary, and I can see her countenance has changed. She seems anxious. The room, which only moments before had a festive air, has a quiet unease. Mr. O puts down his glass and looks at Mary.

Her lower lip is quivering, and finally she asks in a whisper, "When can I see him? Is he close by?"

Mr. O goes over to her and puts his arm around her. "He's on his way now. He'll be here shortly."

"Will I recognize him?" she asks, beginning to cry.

"Of course you will. Look here." Suddenly one of the walls opens up, and I see a tree-lined, cobblestone pathway like something you would see in the American Deep South, with Spanish moss hanging overhead and flowers lining the edges of the walk.

"It's beautiful," Mary says, breathlessly.

Mr. O nods pleasantly. "Yes, it is." He points down the path, and I can see a figure approaching in the distance.

"There he is now," Mr. O announces as he takes Mary by the hand and walks her toward the opening in the wall of the Waiting Room.

"Is that really him?" she whispers, nervously, leaning in toward Mr. O.

"Yes, it's really him—your Kevin."

Mary can only mouth the words because she is crying again. "My Kevin..." But these are tears of joy. She holds tightly on to Mr. O's arm, leaning into him.

I see Kevin walking briskly toward us, and as he gets closer, he starts running. He's holding a bouquet of flowers.

"Kevin!" Mary cries out, uncontrollably.

"Go," Mr. O says, letting go of her and gently nudging her onto the path.

Mary looks back at me for a quick second, smiles, and mouths a "Thank you." Then she runs toward Kevin—the son she lost so long ago, the son who was taken from her, the son she never knew.

I almost forget to breathe. What I'm seeing unfold in front of me seems so surreal, and yet here it is.

In an instant, Kevin reaches his mother—the mother he never knew. Dropping the flowers, he picks her up in his arms, holding her tight as he whirls her around. They are both crying and laughing.

He twirls her again and sets her down gently on the path.

Mary takes his face in her hands, and they look deeply at each other.

"Kevin, it's really you… It's really you." She stands on her toes and kisses his forehead.

Kevin bends down to scoop up the flowers and then presents them to Mary—his mother—who takes them and relishes their scent.

"How beautiful," she says.

"They have a lot of catching up to do," Mr. O says. "It's time to let them have some privacy."

With that, as if on cue somehow, Mary and Kevin turn toward us. "Thank you, Bob!" Mary cries out, waving one hand over her head at me.

Kevin waves a goodbye too.

"Thank you, Mr. O, for not giving up on me," Mary says.

I watch as they take their first steps together up the walkway, hand in hand, unhurried.

At this point I am crying while I watch them, the portal in

the Waiting Room slowly closing. But I savor one last glimpse of mother and son reunited at last. No more brokenness, no more pain, no more death.

I fall to the floor and weep at the goodness that is here—the healing I just witnessed taking place and the sadness that is vanquished forever, replaced for all time by unspeakable joy.

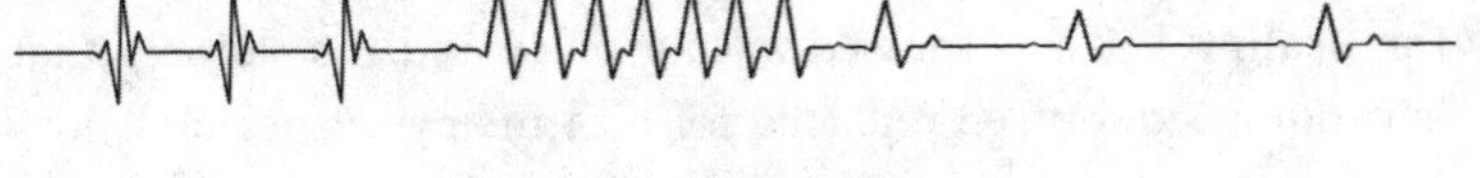

# 15
# THE TWOFER

THE WAITING ROOM has returned to normal, as if anything in this place is normal: talking birds; secret tunnels of foreboding; walls that open up to beautiful tree-lined paths; my boyhood dog, Timber, talking to me; scrumptious, out-of-this-world food; and of course the Way-Back Machine. I'm still wondering how it all works.

I'm back in my chair, facing Mr. O. He's looking at one of the files from the large folder that has reappeared on the desk. I wonder what he can possibly come up with. Part of me wishes this was over, yet another part is eager to clear the decks of any and all unforgiveness—just the memory of outer darkness sends a shiver through me.

"You're doing really well," Mr. O says with gusto, peering at me from behind his spectacles, which have again fallen toward the end of his nose.

"Thanks," I reply cheerily, feeling encouraged at his praise.

Mr. O is sifting through some of the pages from the file. "Let's do a twofer!"

"A twofer?" I have no idea what he's hinting at.

"Yes, a twofer. There are two events here," he says as he pats the file, "that are years apart. The first one is the root, and the second sort of seals the deal, if you catch my drift."

I must have a blank look on my face because he asks, "Do you want to see?"

For a moment, I want to remind Mr. O that I have no choice in the matter, but he beats me to it.

"You're right. You have no choice in the matter!"

"OK, then. I'm ready…I think."

"Good, then let's get started. I'll give you a heads-up. The first event happened when you were in fourth grade and the second in high school just before your sixteenth birthday."

"OK…fourth grade…" I'm trying to think of anything that far back that would have affected me, but before I get very far, Mr. O waves his hand over the Way-Back, and I see my fourth-grade class. I'm a young boy, standing alone in the classroom. It's recess time, so I go down the stairs to the playground. Outside, it's a beautiful spring day. The sun is peeking through the leaves on the trees that border the playground. I hear laughter coming from an area under one of the large oak trees. I wonder what it is, and then suddenly the memory surfaces. I shudder and sink into my chair.

"It's OK, Bob," Mr. O assures me.

"I had forgotten about this. It was so long ago." I shudder again.

"I know, but as I said, this is the root."

"The root to what?"

"The root to your unbelief in God…in all of this." He gestures around the Waiting Room.

I think for a moment and then slowly nod.

"Take a look."

I see myself as a boy walking toward the crowd of older boys who are laughing at something, although I have no idea what.

The boys are all older and taller than me. I get close to them, but I still can't see what's going on. Finally, there's an opening, and I squeeze my way to the front. One of the boys, who appears to be the leader, is bending down to pick up a frog. As I look closer, I can see that the frog is injured, as one of its legs is dangling from its body. At first I think maybe the boys are here to help the injured frog, but that thought vanishes as the ringleader throws the frog straight up into the air. The other boys are pointing to the frog as it reaches its highest point and then falls back to the asphalt on the playground. It lands with a loud smack, and all the boys laugh.

I am stunned, shocked, confused. Why would they do such a cruel thing? I run away as fast as I can back to my classroom. Then I run to the coatroom, bury my face in my jacket, and cry.

"This event really impacted you, didn't it?" Mr. O asks softly.

I'm biting my lower lip, and my stomach is in knots.

He continues, "This is the root of your turning away from the Lord."

"How so?"

"This event made you question why God would allow such cruelty. In your fourth-grade mind, there was no reason for it. Why would He allow it? Why didn't He save the poor frog?"

I nod. "You're right. It's coming back now that you've shown it to me. The incident shocked me to the core, although I couldn't articulate it as a young boy…but you're right. This was the beginning of my unbelief. In some ways it shattered my innocence."

"Yes, exactly. That's why you ran into the coatroom to get as far away as you possibly could from what you were seeing. But there's more here, as I'll show you. Do you recognize where you are now?"

I see the scene shift on the large screen in front of me. There I am in one of my high school study halls that met in the library. I am transfixed by an oversized book on the desk, and I'm just staring at a black-and-white photograph.

"Why?" I ask.

"Remember what I told you: There is a cosmic war raging throughout the universe. It is between those beings who fell from their first estate and did the unthinkable and those who remained faithful and loyal to El Shaddai, the Most High God. The Fallen Ones, who left their first estate, heaven, mingled their seed with the seed of men. They abandoned their rightful place. Remember, these messengers had free will just like you do. But they sided with a being that I refer to as the Dragon. He was corrupted from the beginning and set in motion all that you see before you. Death and fear are his calling cards. He was a murderer from the beginning, and the father of lies. In him is no truth at all. At this moment he still rules the earth, but not for much longer. There will be a cosmic regime change soon." A tired smile touches Mr. O's lips.

I think about what Mr. O has said. Then I point to the picture on the Way-Back; it's frozen, but I know what I'm looking at.

"Why?" I ask again.

Mr. O sighs, long and heavy. "Before I answer this, think about Mary. She was transformed before your eyes. She forgave what held her in bondage. Do you remember this passage from your Bible: '*He will wipe every tear from their eyes. There will be no more death or mourning or crying or pain, for the old order of things has passed away*'?"[1]

"Yes, but I never took much notice of it. It seems like an impossibility."

"But you saw Mary, didn't you? Everything was set right. She was restored. Death was defeated, and now she is in heaven, and the things of the past have fallen of their own weight. There will be no memory of them."

"I believe that. I saw it. She was transformed. She was made whole and filled with joy."

"That's what happens up here. Inexplicable joy!"

I point to the Way-Back. "How can you possibly fix that? How can you reconcile six million Jews murdered in the

Holocaust—their lives taken from them for no other reason than that they were Jewish? How can you reconcile this? And yes, this was the reason I lost my faith in God. How can a loving God allow this? My friend Fred, who was also my pastor, tried to explain it, but unfortunately, he didn't do a very good job, so we agreed not to talk about it."

"What if I were to tell you that every man, woman, and child whose life was taken from them in the Holocaust is here? These are the souls that are under the altar. They are awaiting judgment for their lives being taken from them, and judgment will happen in time."

I am stunned by this revelation. "I've never heard this before."

"And you won't because most people have a misunderstanding of who God is. He is love—a loving God who is both just and holy. His people, the Jews, have a special journey and are different from any other tribe on earth. Even though many of them have rejected their Messiah, Jesus, there will come a time when '*they shall look upon [Him] whom they have pierced, and they shall mourn for him, as one mourneth for his only son.*'"[2]

Mr. O shuts down the Way-Back, and in its place is my wheel floating next to the table. It slowly turns, and to my astonishment I see a dark spoke. There is no picture at the end of the spoke, unlike all the others.

"How come there isn't a picture?"

Mr. O frowns. "'*Thou shalt not make unto thee any graven image.*' Look again." He points to the wheel.[3]

I look over, and I can make out a faint image of a man's face. "What am I looking at?"

"God's calling card."

"I don't understand. It's just a faint image I can barely make out."

"Look again."

I look over at the image, and it slowly changes; I can see a face emerging. "It looks like…is it Jesus?"

"It is."

"What is this? Where does it come from? How come I've never seen this before?"

"The face you are looking at is from the Shroud of Turin. I call it *God's calling card.*"

"I've heard of this but always thought it was a forgery."

"No, it's forensic evidence of the greatest event in all of history—the resurrection of the One who is fully God and fully man, Jesus. Are you aware that until it was photographed in 1898, no one had ever seen it?"

I shake my head with my eyes fixed on Mr. O.

"The image you see is a *negative* image on the cloth, and when photographed, it reveals all the details of the passion of the Christ, the Messiah."

"So how do I light up this spoke?"

"You have to forgive the boys with the frog, and then you have to forgive God for what you perceive as an irreconcilable event—the Holocaust. The boys with the frog were the root, and seeing the atrocities of the Holocaust pushed you over the edge. You lost your faith."

"I did, but later Fred helped me get it back…sort of."

Mr. O nods. "He did, but you still have doubts, and this is why the darkness is there." He pauses. "You know what you need to do."

"How can I forgive God?"

"The same way you forgave the others. But you also have to forgive yourself."

"Myself?"

"Yes, yourself. You feel guilty about the whole affair, so even the lack of your faith can be forgiven here. You know what to do. Light up the wheel. Remember, I told you this was a twofer, and now you know why."

I let out a deep sigh. Overwhelmed, I look over at the wheel, and there is the faint outline of a face. I watch as it changes into the image Mr. O told me was on the Shroud of Turin. Looking at it sends a shiver through my body—through my soul. I close my eyes, bow my head, and do the work I must do. A moment later I can feel something deep within my soul break free. My body trembles as I sense something leave my body. I feel like a tremendous weight has been lifted from me. I glance over to see the spoke is lit up! Then I look at the face of Jesus, and I'm astounded to see the face come alive and wink at me!

"Way to go!" Mr. O exclaims, laughing.

"Did you see that? He winked at me!"

"That's because He loves you. He's proud of you, and He will never forsake you or abandon you."

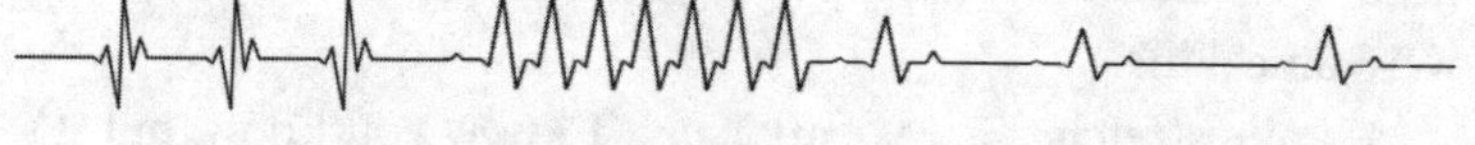

# 16
# SKIING POWDER

Y EVER-BRIGHTENING WHEEL has once again vanished, and I'm still trying to grasp that the picture of Jesus from the Shroud of Turin came alive and winked at me.

I've learned at least one thing being in the Waiting Room: Mr. O is unpredictable, and you never know what will happen next. The rules I was accustomed to on earth don't apply here; I suppose that's an understatement. However, the frog incident has been reconciled, and it no longer has power over me. Once again I feel a lightness in my soul and wonder if I'll float up to the ceiling, as before.

I look up to see Mr. O smiling at me. He can somehow read my thoughts, and sure enough he says, "'*All things work together for good to them that love God.*'"[1]

Mr. O clears his throat as he leans forward in his chair. "Even to those souls who perished at the hands of the Nazis. As I told you, these are some of the martyrs who, through the centuries, died for their faith. These are under the altar and are protected for eternity."

I nod my head at what Mr. O has explained. It is very sobering, but the implications are mind-numbing.

Suddenly, Mr. O says, "I think you need a break."

"What do you mean, a break?"

"You've been through a lot while you've been here, and you need a break. What was your favorite thing to do when you were on earth?"

A smile stretches across my face. "I know you know, but it's skiing. I love to ski!"

"Exactly. And you're going to go skiing now."

"What? There's no snow…no groomed slopes…no winter!"

"That's what you think. Watch."

On the table in front of me I see what looks like a miniature mountain covered with snow. "Hey, that looks like Arapahoe Basin in Colorado. It's one of my favorite places to ski! But it's in miniature."

"Exactly. 'A-Basin,' as the locals call it, and you've got it all to yourself."

I jump up from my chair and examine the miniature ski slope that has just appeared on the table. "It's so small," I say, chuckling. "But there are the chairlifts! The snow's been groomed, and there's not a single skier on my favorite run!"

"Not for long." Mr. O's eyes twinkle. "Are you ready?"

"Ready for what?" I have no idea what he's hinting at.

"To go do your favorite thing…ski!"

I laugh out loud. "How's that going to happen? I'm way too big for this miniature slope that you somehow created. I appreciate what you're trying to do, but—"

Before I can get the rest of the sentence out of my mouth, I find myself on the mountain, standing at the chairlift. I have skis on, and I'm dressed in my good ski parka and powder bibs. I look upward to see where Mr. O is, but I can't see him. "How did you…? Never mind," I blurt out, grinning.

The chairlift is running. I see it coming toward me, so I take a few steps and get ready to board it. The next thing I know, I'm going up the mountain. I'm getting excited. I love this mountain and have skied on this slope and gone up this chair many times. I ride to the top of the lift and get off. Before you can say "*Jean-Claude Killy,*" I'm off down the slope. The snow is amazing! I make a few slow turns, and then I go for it down the fall line. My body moves in a steady rhythm, making quick turns left, right, left. The slope is about to go into a steep part, so I dig my edges in and lean into the hill. I can almost touch the slope with my hand.

"Woo-hoo!" I yell as the steep part ends. I'm moving really fast through what skiers call "cruisers," wide, open terrains with a gentle slope. I'm skiing close to the edge where the pine trees are. The snow is crisp, and on the edges there's still about four inches of fresh powder. It's like floating down the mountain.

I reach the bottom and ski over to the chairlift. Of course, there's no line, and for a few moments, I forget about the Waiting Room. I have my own private ski slope! Who could imagine such a thing? I hop on the chair, and then I'm up above the slopes again. It's a perfect bluebird day, and it makes me recall my ski buddy who has the same name as mine, Bob. We used to joke about our names being the same. We've skied this mountain many times together. Good ol' Ski Buddy Bob.

The chair is at the top of the slope again. I hop off and start down a long run, a cruiser. I'm just relishing every turn, the layer of fresh powder beneath my skis, the crisp clean air, the wind in my face, and the sun overhead. I'm in heaven. And then it dawns on me…wait a second, I really am in heaven… sort of…but I'm in the Waiting Room! Then I say out loud, "I wish Bob, my ski buddy, was here to enjoy this with me."

I finish up the cruiser run and get in the chairlift, positioning myself to take yet another run.

"Do you mind if I join you?" a voice calls from behind me.

I turn around to see Mr. O in a racing ski suit, with patches and pins of ski resorts from all over the world.

"Mr. O! How did you get here?"

He laughs and takes a few steps on his skis so he's next to me. Then the chair comes around, and we both hop on together. He points to one of the pins on his racing suit. "It's one of my favorites."

I lean over to get a better look. "That's the Telluride pin! I've skied there too."

"I'm aware, and we could have gone there, but I know you're partial to A-Basin."

I nod.

"Yes, I love this place! Skiing makes me forget everything. I am one with the snow!" I laugh.

The chair arrives at the top, and we both get off.

"I'll race you!" Mr. O shouts. Before I can answer, he's skating toward the slope and picking up speed.

"You're on!" I start skating too, pushing with my poles and using my skis like ice skates. I'm starting to close the gap, and then we're on top of the slope. Mr. O heads to the middle of the slope, crouches down, and takes off right down the fall line.

"Not so fast, Citizen!" I shout as I get into a tuck position on my skis. The wind is whistling in my ears, and I'm beginning to close the distance. Mr. O hits a jump and is airborne. He lands and, for a second, seems like he'll lose his balance, but he recovers. A moment later I hit the jump, and instantly I'm in the air! I make a smooth landing and tuck even lower on my skis.

We're about halfway down the mountain, and I'm gaining on him. But then I catch one of my edges and lose control. I finally regain my position, but it's put me out of the race. Now Mr. O has pulled way ahead of me.

"You win!" I shout, pushing off to catch up with him.

I watch as Mr. O makes a long turn and comes to a graceful stop.

I'm headed toward him, and as I stop, I spray him with snow from my skis.

"Nice, Bob," he says with a laugh, wiping the snow off his racing suit.

"I almost had you, but I caught an edge, and that was it!"

Mr. O nods. "Let's do another, shall we?"

"Absolutely!"

We head toward the lift and wait for the chair to make its turn so we can hop on.

Once again we are lifted high above the perfectly groomed slopes below us.

Silent, we are both in the moment, relishing the sunlight, the bluebird sky above us, the snow-covered boughs of the pine trees, the invigorating air.

"I could stay here forever." I beam, blissfully.

"So could I. In some ways it doesn't get better than this," he says. "However, we have work to do."

I nod, feeling refreshed, and inhale deeply, filling my lungs with all the rejuvenating fresh air I can.

"You know, Bob, you're doing the right thing; you're on the right track. Keep doing what you're doing."

"You mean with lighting up the wheel, right?"

"Exactly. Forgiveness is your ticket to a season ski pass—for eternity."

We reach the top of the lift and get off.

"That's a long time, eternity." I'm trying to grasp even the concept. "I can't imagine what that's like."

"Well, I can tell you this: It goes on forever." He chuckles.

"Is there skiing there? You know, once I'm out of the Waiting Room, can you ski in heaven?"

Mr. O nods, smiling. "What if I told you that it takes over a week of earth time to do one run on some of the slopes!"

"Seriously?"

"You'll be on them before you know it. But we still have work to do, so after this run, we should get back to it."

And with that Mr. O pushes with his poles and heads down a cruiser run.

I follow him, relishing each moment—leaning into the upslope, keeping my skis perfectly together, and turning with ease on the soft powder.

Mr. O slows down a little. We are skiing side by side, then crisscrossing each other's tracks and playing follow the leader. Finally, we reach the bottom, and there we are in the Waiting Room again—with our skis still on!

"That was incredible," I say. I look over to the table, and the miniature mountain is gone. In its place is my file. I wonder what we'll tackle next.

"Just lean your skis against the wall, and we'll pick up where we left off."

We lean our skis against the wall with the "*Escape Tunnel*" sign overhead and make our way back to the table.

"That was really fun," I say. "Thank you for doing that for me."

"Well, you needed a break, and I was glad to do it. The snow was perfect, wasn't it?"

"Couldn't have been better."

"Remember, you're on the right track. So keep doing what you're doing, and in no time you'll have your season pass!"

And with that Mr. O pulls a few pages from the file.

# 17
# BETRAYAL

"THIS NEXT ONE is tough, but I know you can do it." Mr. O waves his hand, and there is my wheel. Lots of spokes have lit up because of the work we're doing in the Waiting Room. Others are still very dark. Mr. O points at one of them. My eyes follow the spoke to the end, and I see a picture of my first wife, Susan. She looks angry.

"I can't believe I have to deal with this," I gripe as my smile, fully charged with snow and sunshine, melts into a scowl.

"Of course you can believe it! Look at everything you've been through and all the spokes you've lit up. Keep doing what you're doing. You're on the right track. You're doing the right thing."

I take a deep breath and sigh. "This *is* a tough one."

"In some respects, they're all tough. But remember, forgiveness is the key that allows you to leave the Waiting Room and explore what's outside these walls. I've let you see just some of what awaits you."

"That's true. The path Kevin was on when he met his mother was the most beautiful place I have ever seen."

"That's only the tip of the iceberg," Mr. O says, grinning, "to use an overused phrase, but it's true. You have no idea of the wonders that are here."

"She cheated on me!" I blurt out.

Unfazed, Mr. O says, "Yes, she did, and your point is?"

I'm getting mad now. "Are you serious? That's your response? She cheated on me. She went out with my copilot, who at the time was my *best friend*! And by the way, he was married! So it was a real mess."

"Yes, I'm aware of the details," Mr. O says as he pats the file next to him. "You've harbored a lot of bitterness and unforgiveness toward her for decades—dare I say toward both of them?"

I catch myself wanting to say, "*But I'm justified.*" Instead, I take a deep breath. "You're right, but it's just not fair. It took me over a year before I was able to even think about dating another woman. The fallout from it affected every part of me. I almost didn't make it and thought about…thought about…"

"It's OK, Bob, I know. You were thinking about suicide."

I hang my head in shame and exhale slowly. "Yes, I toyed with it, but I couldn't do it. I was too afraid of what would happen afterward."

"You think that it was the unpardonable sin?"

"You're in my head again! I never really understood what that meant, 'the unpardonable sin.' I always thought suicide was the big one that puts you over the edge."

"The Lord on high can forgive everything except the unpardonable sin, which is renouncing or blaspheming the Holy Spirit—the Spirit of the living God. That's *the* really big no-no. So suicide is not the unpardonable sin; however, it's not the best path to choose. It hurts everyone involved. The repercussions have a deep ripple effect and linger for years or even decades. It can affect a generation far into the future. This is part of what the Dragon does. He makes a person's situation look hopeless and then presents suicide as the way out. In essence, the Dragon is stealing that person's life and thus negating what they may have accomplished if they had only stuck it out."

"I never thought of it that way."

"True, but this is why it's *not* the unpardonable sin—the sin that if someone commits it, there's no way out, no forgiveness. So let's get back to Susan. She left you for another man, your best friend. They cheated on you, they betrayed your trust, and they essentially stabbed you in the back. That act shattered your soul, as you know that when you marry someone, there is a soul connection. Susan violated that. It's like taking a rock and throwing it at a plate-glass window or like a marble in a slingshot aimed at the window." The corners of Mr. O's lips go up just slightly.

I bite my lower lip. "I never thought of it that way. That's why I felt so shattered. A part of me was ripped away by her actions."

"And what about your so-called friend and captain of the plane you copiloted, Tom." He glances at the file. "You never spoke to him again; you took a sabbatical from flying and then signed up with another airline to avoid ever seeing him again."

"Yes, I never saw either of them again. It's like they vanished off the face of the earth, and I'm glad I never saw them together."

"And you still harbor bitterness, anger, and unforgiveness toward them, even after all these years."

I nod slowly, wondering how this is going to play out. But I know one thing from all this—here in the Waiting Room with Mr. O—there's *no way* I'm going back into the Escape Tunnel. I'm going to forgive because I know what happens if I don't. Yet I can't find a path to it. At least not at the moment.

Finally, I reply, "You're right. The whole affair is still there as if it were yesterday. For the most part, I've blocked it out. I have my Evelyn by my side, who has been faithful and who still loves me. My marriage has been good. It's made me forget about what happened almost forty years ago."

Mr. O becomes very serious and looks directly at me, unblinking. "You thought about killing them both?"

I let out a deep sigh, looking away at the wall and then at the floor. "I did. I won't lie to you. But of course, I never acted on it. I was betrayed by my first wife and my so-called best friend, a man I looked up to. My life was ripped apart. It became a mess."

"And the whole mess, as you call it, festered for years. You did talk to Fred, your pastor and good friend, about it, which helped. And yet…"

I pick up the thread. "And yet I never forgave either of them. Aren't there some situations where you don't have to forgive? Isn't there a get-out-of-forgiving card? You know it's not fair."

Mr. O leans toward me and reminds me, whispering, "What about when Jesus was on the cross? He looks down at those who have tortured and abused Him, and what does He say? '*Father, forgive them; for they know not what they do.*' How was that fair?"[1]

I feel that in my gut. "You're right about the festering. Even though it was decades ago, it creeps up from time to time. I've learned to push it out of my mind and not engage it. But it always comes back—always."

"I understand all too well. Some memories never go away. They cling to a person's soul, their spirit, their mind. They linger in their dreams, and then triggers in everyday life bring them rushing to the surface."

"Life is just not fair at all."

"I agree. It's part of what happened way back in the garden. Sin and death entered the world through the Dragon and his cleverly crafted deception. Every person who has ever walked the earth has a part of their soul and spirit broken and shattered, and some never regain wholeness again. That's what Adam and Eve traded their innocence for: a lie.

"Everyone who has ever lived has brokenness. Some hide it better than others. Some walk through life with a fake smile on their face. Some bury themselves in work or sports to try to cover up their brokenness. Some turn to drugs and others to pornography. The list is endless. Only when a person realizes they are running from the festering wounds are they able to be healed. Even that isn't 100 percent, as the memory will return. The good news is this: When human beings turn to me, I can heal them."

"I remember hearing that, but I thought that was Jesus speaking."

Mr. O nods with a twinkle in his eye. "Yes, I was quoting what Jesus said. But Susan and Tom still need to be forgiven. And remember, in no way does your forgiveness justify their actions. I can tell you something—something I usually don't do here in the Waiting Room. Susan and Tom's marriage was birthed in a lie, and just so you know—you're not allowed to gloat, but it might make forgiving them easier—they are two very unhappy people. Once the passion and the sex wore off, as well as the thrill of cheating, they were faced with discovering who each other really was. It didn't go well, and they never had children. As I told you, I usually don't give out this information, but in your case it will help. They are two very miserable people. Of course, I don't wish this on anyone, but that's the case. They both know deep in their souls that their marriage was born in a lie and deception."

Mr. O leans back in his chair and folds his hands behind his head. "Do you want me to give you a few minutes alone?"

I shake my head. "No, I got this. I know what I have to do." I take a deep breath and blow it out. "And in some ways, I'm looking forward to it. I don't want this hanging over my head and festering in my soul anymore. I realize that it's not worth it."

Mr. O smiles and nods in agreement. "Forgiving is not some magic antidote to the hurts that people experience while living, but it sets what I call 'supernatural healing' into motion. It calls on a power that is higher than the unforgiveness and higher than the hurt, and *then* there is supernatural healing. Most people don't realize the healing has taken place because it's subtle and sometimes happens slowly. But at some point most people realize that the hurt, the pain, and the memory are no longer haunting them. And by the way, *haunting* is a good word to use. They are healed, at least as much as a person can be healed while on earth. Of course, it's different here. There is no more pain, no more suffering, and no more hauntings. The former things have passed away—even the memory of them."

Suddenly the light in the room grows dim. The only light is from the wheel hovering above the floor of the Waiting Room next to me.

"I'm going to leave you for a bit so you can work this out by yourself." Mr. O gets up from his chair and then says again, "You're doing the right thing. You're on the right track. Keep doing what you're doing." He lays his hand on my shoulder, giving it a slight squeeze, and leaves the room.

I'm alone in the Waiting Room, and all is quiet. I take a deep breath and begin the work I need to do. I am forgiving the wrongs that were done to me, and this time I go a step further. I am actually blessing Susan and Tom—I'm blessing them and wishing them goodwill.

In some ways I can't believe I'm doing this, but here in the Waiting Room, the events that have held me captive—for that's what I have become, a captive to my own bitterness and unforgiveness—are falling off me, falling from their own weight. They're fleeing from me because they no longer have power over me.

The room grows brighter, and I look over at the wheel and notice that Susan's spoke has lit up. I can see that she's there, but her head is lowered as if in shame. I wonder how that can be, and then I say out loud to her picture at the end of the spoke, "It's OK, Susan. Be blessed. You are forgiven."

The shame is now gone, and I can see she's smiling. All is well. I'm on the right track, as Mr. O likes to say. I say to myself, "I'll keep doing what I'm doing. I'm doing the right thing!"

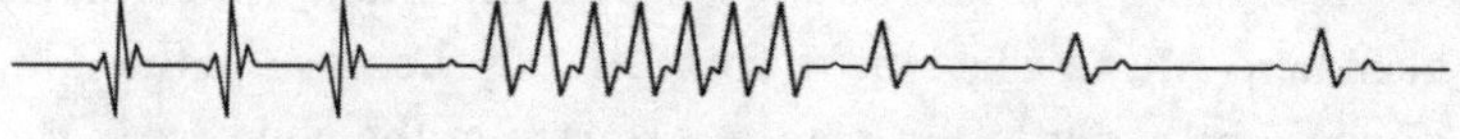

# 18
# A SURPRISE VISITOR

THERE'S A KNOCK on the door to the Waiting Room. I'm wondering who could possibly be knocking other than Mr. O. I'm not sure what to do. I pause for a moment, and then the knock repeats.

"Come in?" My response is more of a question, because I'm not sure what's going on.

The door opens slowly, and a young man around twenty-five years old enters.

He has brown hair and blue eyes that sparkle. He slowly closes the door behind him and steps into the room. He's looking at me, and his face is radiating joy and love. I have no idea who he is.

"Hi, Dad," he says softly.

With those words a dam breaks in my heart and soul, and I leap out of the chair toward him. "Luke! Luke! It's really you… It's really you!"

I throw my arms around him, weeping uncontrollably as I keep whispering his name. Then I take his precious face in my hands and kiss his cheek.

"You're all grown up," I say, trying to get the words past my lips frozen in a wide smile.

"Yes, Dad, that's what happens up here, just like with your Aunt Mary."

"You know about that?"

"Yes, and I've been rooting for you the whole time you've been here. Mr. O asked me to come see you, because he thought it would be easier to forgive if we started at the good part: Me seeing you here. Then we'd work backward."

"You have no idea what it means to me to see you again. If only your mother were here." I hug him again. "The last time I saw you, you were so frail, gaunt, pale, and dying. And then you left us. Your mom never really got over it, and I pushed it as far back in my mind as I could."

"Yeah, I know. But everything is made new here, as Mr. O says—whole, hale, and hearty."

"You certainly look great and all grown-up," I repeat, overwhelmed.

Luke asks, "Can I tell you something?"

"Anything, son."

"The last time you saw me—right before I passed away from leukemia—I told you not to worry, that the angels were there in the hospital room. Do you remember?"

I nod with the mingled joy and pain so tangible it feels like I've got one foot in Luke's hospital room.

He continues, "Well, they were there just like I told you, and they took me right to Jesus. He held me in His arms and comforted me. Then He spent some time showing me around. While this was going on, I was growing from the frail boy into the man you see now. I don't know how much time I spent with Jesus, but He told me a lot of things. When He thought I was ready, He assigned one of His messengers to guide me and show me some things I needed to learn."

I nod my head, amazed at what I'm hearing.

"And I came in thirty-fourth in the men's archery competition!"

"What?" The whole room feels electrified, and I don't know whether I can comprehend any more.

Luke laughs. "You remember how I loved archery at summer camp, but then I got sick and that was the end of that."

"I remember," I say, quietly.

"Well, I was assigned a personal trainer. He was a Scythian warrior. He basically grew up with a bow and arrow centuries before I was born. He could ride a horse and hit his mark at 50 yards away. Anyway, he trained me, and when the competition was held, I placed 34th out of the men! And listen to this: Overall, I was 568th, which is incredible because I was competing against the angels!"

"The angels?" I'm dumbfounded at what I'm hearing.

"They've had eons to practice, and they never miss. I mean, *never.* It comes down to fractions of an inch with each shot in the competition. Sometimes it takes hours to decide on one shot. It's that close! But I did really good against them."

"There's an archery competition here? That's—"

"Incredible?" Mr. O says, finishing my thought again as he enters the Waiting Room. "I see you two have met again." He beams. "How wonderful."

I nod but get back to the topic. "Archery competition?"

Luke laughs. "Yep, thirty-fourth in the men's division, and I was competing against world-class, um, I should say, '*heavenly-class* warriors.'"

I'm not sure what to say, but I manage, "That's wonderful. Congrats, son!"

Mr. O exclaims, "Yes, by all means, congratulations are in order. Life is so full here that there's almost no time to take it all in. But you have eternity to explore, create, and think about anything and everything you have an inkling toward—the possibilities are endless. Sorry, I gave that saying to one of your ad agencies on earth, but it's true. They are limitless. You have freedom to create, explore, and learn."

Luke chimes in. "Like learning from one of the best archers in history. His white stone name is Venbar. He came in first place in the contest. I still meet with him."

This is all just too much to take in. I haven't seen Luke since he died in the hospital room years ago. A skeleton covered by a white sheet. His hair almost gone, his cheeks sunken, his eyes feverish. Then he slipped away quietly while Evelyn and I were sleeping in chairs next to him—we never saw his last moment. The nurse awakened us. When Evelyn saw that he had passed, she wouldn't let go of him. She held Luke in her arms and rocked him, crying softly. The doctor came with more nurses, and they gave Evelyn something to calm her down, and finally—after almost an hour—she put Luke back on the bed, kissed his forehead one last time, and left the room.

I have pushed all this into a private compartment never to be opened or looked at—never. Even when Luke's birthday came around, I would avoid it, but Evelyn never forgot and would have a cake. As Mr. O said earlier, some wounds never heal.

"Well, Luke, thank you for coming and helping your dad in the Waiting Room. We have to take care of some business though, and I think your father would like the privacy."

"I understand," Luke replies. He gives me one more hug, and I don't want to let go of him. He heads to the door, where he turns one last time and gives me a thumbs-up. Then he's gone.

"Thank you for letting me see him again," I say. "I don't know how to thank you enough. It almost doesn't seem possible, yet here he was. I held him, and he's all grown!"

"Yes, all things are made new—all things. But we have some work to do."

The large wheel appears. I look at the spokes, and Mr. O points to the one with Luke and the doctors.

"I know where this is going."

"Good for you," Mr. O says.

"I never forgave the doctors or one of the couples at church whose daughter was going through leukemia at the same time. She made it, and Luke died."

"I know." Mr. O's voice is compassionate.

"Pastor Fred would pray for Luke and the other couple's daughter, Katie. The whole church would join in. *Amens* would echo off the church walls. It felt good, and it gave us hope—something to believe in. Maybe, just maybe, God would step in and heal him. I suppose with Katie, He did, but not with Luke."

"You were mad at God *again*," Mr. O says, softly.

"Very much so. And you can add to that the doctors who poisoned Luke with their 'medicine,' the nurses with their endless needles, and the well-meaning people at church, including Fred, who said they were sorry for our loss once we lost Luke."

"That's the reason I had Luke come see you, which is something I usually don't do. But as you can see, there are exceptions."

I exhale a deep sigh. "Thanks again, Mr. O, it helped a lot to see him again. And thirty-fourth in archery...wow."

"Once we finish here, you'll be watching him at the archery meets soon enough."

Smiling, I nod in reply.

"But let's get back to the wheel. At the end of the spoke, you can see everyone is in a group shot: the doctors, nurses, Fred, and others. They're all waiting for you to forgive."

After a beat of silence, I have to ask, "Why did God heal Katie and not Luke?"

Mr. O says, "How do you know He didn't heal them both? But in Luke's case, it just wasn't the way you would have imagined. Remember, He can see all of time at a glance. Maybe there was something in Luke's future that He spared him from. Maybe that's why He took him when He did."

My hands are folded on my lap, and I'm hunched over in my chair, staring at the table and trying to get my head around what Mr. O is saying. "This is too much for me. I'm just a stupid man."

"Man, yes; stupid, no."

I let out a long exhale again.

Mr. O continues, "Think of it this way. People look at life one moment at a time. They can't see the future. They are stuck in the space-time continuum. God is *outside* time, as you can see by being here in the Waiting Room. How long do you think you've been here? Hours, days, weeks?"

"I don't know. I hadn't thought about that." But now I am.

"Think of all you've accomplished since you've been here, and yet you're not weary, are you? Time—as you know it—doesn't exist here. You can see that everything is made whole here for those who are admitted. And just so you know, not everyone gets in. '*But the cowardly, unbelieving, abominable, murderers, sexually immoral, sorcerers, idolaters, and all liars shall have their part in the lake which burns with fire and brimstone, which is the second death.*'"[1]

"No hope for them?"

Mr. O shakes his head soberly. "They have made a choice and will not turn lest they be healed. And just so you know, they could be healed."

"It was so good to see Luke. I don't have the words to describe it."

"I know. Think about how Mary, the mother of Jesus, felt when she saw Him after He had conquered death and rose from the grave. Can you even imagine?"

I nod, pondering the thought.

He continues, "She knew who He was and thought He would save Himself and come down from the cross, but she didn't know the plan that defeated the Dragon. No one saw it—not Mary, not the disciples. As I told you earlier, how can you kill God? You can't. And yet Jesus is fully God and fully man. His body lay in the tomb for three days while His spirit and soul went to sheol, where He proclaimed to the fallen angels locked away in gloomy dungeons that there was no 'jailbreak' coming for them. It is the most cosmic event in the universe!

"At any rate," he goes on, "sometimes His ways are beyond a human's comprehension. Remember, He knows everything, and Luke is here. You saw him. Thirty-fourth is pretty good, huh?"

I smile. "You can say that again. I get it."

"I'm going to leave again. Sometimes it's good for a man to be alone to wrestle with his soul."

With that Mr. O leaves the room.

I glance over at the wheel, looking at the group of doctors, nurses, church people, and everyone involved. Then I do what I am here to do: I forgive.

# 19
# CITY UNDER CONSTRUCTION

MR. O IS back in the room, and I can tell he's up to something. He's got a mischievous smile that makes his eyes squint with hidden merriment.

"How would you like a bird's-eye view of the New Jerusalem?"

"What?"

"The New Jerusalem. It's fairly large, and you won't be able to see it all, but I can show you some of it."

"I thought the New Jerusalem was just an allegory. You mean, it really exists?"

Mr. O gives me one of his indescribable looks that are hard to put into words but somehow speak volumes.

"It's still under construction at the moment, but we're almost finished."

"Under construction? Seriously?"

"What? Do you think God just snaps His fingers and—voilà!—the New Jerusalem appears? He could do that, but the angels would have a fit. Who do you think is building it? They love construction!"

"I never thought about it. Angels?"

"Most people don't, but I can assure you that it's been quite an undertaking. The planning stages alone went on forever." Mr. O chuckles, as if remembering.

"How so?"

"Well, one group insisted on creating a cube-shaped structure, while another group insisted a pyramid shape was the way to go. The arguing went on for who knows how long."

"How long?"

"Far too long. In earth time it was over a century before I finally put a stop to it and made the decision. Otherwise, nothing would get built!" He chuckles again.

"You put a stop to it?"

"I do have other duties that you're not aware of."

"OK." I'm not sure what Mr. O means by his other duties, but I press for more information. "How big is this city then?"

Mr. O sits down and waves his hand over the Way-Back. Suddenly a scale model of the New Jerusalem—superimposed over the United States—appears on the table, showing its enormity.

"It almost spans shore to shore," I stammer.

"The most extensive building project in the history of the known and unknown universe—and done without a building permit!"

I stare in awe. "How is that even possible? It's so big!"

Mr. O laughs. "Fifteen hundred miles in each direction. Think of what we can do with this. Think of how many people it can hold. Think of the possibilities! Do you know that it descends to earth *after* the one-thousand-year millennial reign of the King?"

"I thought all this was an allegory, and there was no literal thousand-year rule by the King. Isn't that Jesus?"

"I can assure you, Bob, this is not the case. The King will return at some point on earth. He will set up His kingdom. It's neither an allegory nor a fantasy—nor the ravings of an old man whose visions are not to be trusted. For *what was written will come to pass; what was foretold will unfold.* The King will return and dwell with men for a thousand years. He will rule the nations with a rod of iron. Then, after the thousand years, the New Jerusalem will descend. How glorious!" he says with a look of anticipation. "Of course, there is one last interlude with the Dragon before it happens, but after that, he will be put down for the last time—forever."

My head is spinning, and I'm not sure what to say. I've never heard this portion of the Bible explained like this.

Mr. O continues, "I'll quote you a passage from the Book of Revelation, which is the revealing of the future. '*I saw heaven standing open and there before me was a white horse, whose rider is called Faithful and True. With justice he judges and wages war. His eyes are like blazing fire, and on his head are many crowns. He has a name written on him that no one knows but he himself. He is dressed in a robe dipped in blood, and his name is the Word of God. The armies of heaven...*'"[1] Mr. O stops and gives me a very serious look. "You're part of this, Bob. You're part of the army—the army of heaven."

I nod dumbly. I have no idea where he's going with this, and it seems like he's jumping from one subject to another. What does this have to do with the New Jerusalem?

He continues, "'*The armies of heaven were following him, riding on white horses and dressed in fine linen, white and clean.*'[2] As I said before, you're in that army, Bob."

I nod, not knowing what else to do or say.

"Now, think of this: The armies of heaven are leaving heaven and coming to earth, specifically at the great battle of Armageddon. The armies of the Dragon have gathered, thinking in their hubris that they can defeat the rider on the white horse—the King—Jesus! How foolish they are." Mr. O suddenly has a faraway look in his eyes. "Remember, Bob, the armies of the King are on white horses." He pauses for effect. "And how do you think those horses get from heaven to earth?"

I shrug.

Mr. O suddenly bolts out of his chair and exclaims, "Those horses can fly! Remember? I told you that."

I'm drawn into Mr. O's excitement.

"And fly they will—and you'll be on one! But let's get back to the New Jerusalem."

He pauses for effect. "Would you like to see what the New Jerusalem looks like at the moment?"

"Yes! But how? We're in the Waiting Room, and other than going to the Escape Tunnel—something I don't ever want to venture into again—how is that possible?"

"Well, why don't we start with a white horse?"

"A white horse?"

Mr. O looks at the wall that opened when Aunt Mary met Kevin. Suddenly it opens again, but this time there is a beautiful field that seems to go on forever with rolling hills and trees. In the field and trotting toward us are two majestic white horses.

"How do you do that?" I ask rhetorically, knowing he isn't going to tell me, but I can at least try.

I look back at the field and notice that one of the horses is larger and perhaps grander than the other.

"The one on the right is mine," Mr. O says, yet again reading my thoughts.

With that he gets up from the table and walks to the opening. I follow, wondering what he's got in store for me.

He raises his hand and greets the horses. They neigh back to him and trot over to us. Mr. O reaches out to his horse, who rubs Mr. O's chest with his head. He whispers something I can't hear in the horse's ear, and the horse whinnies a reply. The other horse approaches me and lowers his head. I'm not sure what to do. I have never been this close to a horse in my life. I hesitantly reach out and touch his white face.

Then I hear in my head, "Hello, Bob!"

Mr. O somehow knows what has just happened. "He knows

who you are, and yes, he can talk to you, just the way your dog Timber did."

Once again I'm trying to process all that's happening, but it's just too much for me to take in.

"Are you ready?" Mr. O asks.

"Ready for what?"

With that Mr. O somehow defies gravity by leaping into the air, and he is now sitting on the back of his horse.

He motions for me to do the same, but I just shrug, not knowing how to mount a horse. Is this really my horse?

"Let me help," I hear someone say in my head. I look at my horse, who is bending his legs down so that he is sitting in front of me.

Then I hear the horse say in my head, "Hop on!"

I'm in shock, but I slowly mount my horse. Once I'm seated on his back, he stands back up again.

"Watch this." Mr. O has that all-too-familiar glint in his eyes again.

Suddenly both horses unfold *their wings*! They weren't there before, but somehow, both horses have wings! How did that just happen?

Mr. O smiles and gives his horse a pat. "Are you ready?"

Neither of these horses has a saddle or bridle. Even though I don't know anything about riding a horse, I've seen enough movies to know that without a saddle or bridle, this isn't going to work out very well, or so I think.

"Your horse will never let you fall off—ever—so you don't have to do anything. Just keep your eyes open and follow me."

Without waiting for a reply, Mr. O's horse takes off. In a few strides, the pair are airborne. Then my horse lunges forward. I grasp his mane in my hands, and after two or more lunges, we're in the air following Mr. O.

I can't believe this is happening!

"Hi-ho, Silver! Away!" Mr. O shouts.

I start laughing at the *Lone Ranger* reference. I'm gobsmacked. I'm on a flying white horse who can talk to me. Seriously?!

We are high above the field, and far in the distance I can see a large pyramid-shaped structure, larger than anything I have ever seen. Our flying white horses are side by side, high above the ground below. Mr. O points to the enormous New Jerusalem.

He calls out, "That's where we're headed. It's still under construction, as I told you, but we're gaining on it, and soon it will be finished."

I look ahead, and the new city is so massive that I'm awestruck. In fact, part of it just disappears into the distance because it's fifteen hundred miles in width and breadth—and the same in height. It is the most beautiful building, if I can call it that, that I have ever seen. We are getting closer now. Because of the grandeur of the city, I have almost forgotten that I am flying toward it on the back of a white horse! I can see that we are headed toward what looks like a gate of some sort. It appears to have been constructed from a giant pearl. A high wall is in front of—what shall I call it?—the new city, and there's a courtyard between the wall and the giant pearl gate.

"That's where we're headed, but we won't land. We'll only fly by because the city has not yet been consecrated."

I have no idea what Mr. O means by this, but I follow his lead. As we approach the city, I can plainly see beings who are mighty-looking men. They must be angels; they have to be. At least fifty of them are going in and out of the one gate we are nearing.

Suddenly all of them stop what they're doing, turn to face us, and cry out in unison, "Hail to the King! Hail to the King! Hail to the King!"

I'm wondering why these angels are saying this, because Mr. O is certainly not a king.

Mr. O waves at the throng and then turns his steed so that

he is parallel to the side of the city. We are now flying down the length of it. It is the most beautiful thing I have ever seen. The walls are a shimmering gold, but somehow I can see through them. It's breathtaking.

We fly for perhaps a minute or two until Mr. O turns away from the city, and I follow. I can see we are headed back the way we came. I let go of my horse's mane because I realize this horse, who called me by name, would never let me fall off it—ever. I relax and feel the wind in my face as the horse's wings slice through the air. It is the most incredible moment I have ever experienced. I don't want it to end, and yet I can see that we are descending back into the field. I can see the white walls of what I know to be the Waiting Room.

Mr. O lands first, and we follow close behind. The horses' wings fold into their bodies again, and we trot over to the entrance of the Waiting Room.

"Well, Bob, what say you?" Mr. O slides off his horse.

"That's the most amazing thing I have ever witnessed…I'm speechless."

Mr. O nods in agreement and, taking his horse's head in his hands, whispers something in his ear.

I dismount and stroke my horse's face.

"I'll be waiting for you, Bob," my horse says to me.

I look into his eyes and see the love the horse has for me. I feel a shiver go down my spine.

"Thank you," I manage to say. Then we're back in the Waiting Room. The wall is closed, and I turn my attention to Mr. O, who once again is sitting at the table.

"Shall we?" He pats the folder, and my wheel appears on cue.

As I'm taking my seat, he says, "Look here." And with that I see another dark spoke.

# 20
# PUZZLE PIECES

I LOOK OVER AT the dark spoke Mr. O is pointing at. As usual, I follow it to see who might be at the end of it, and I recognize the scene immediately. My hackles are raised. "So we're going here!"

Mr. O nods.

"I was in the right, and you know it!" I bluster.

"Yes, you were, and I applaud your heroism. But we need to walk through this; it's complex. By the way, look at the file. You're getting close to finishing things up."

I look at my file, and it's true: The file is shrinking.

"How is this complex?" I bluster. "I was in a fight, I was in the right, and it changed my life."

"Well, let's go through the whole thing on the Way-Back."

I give a deep sigh and mumble, "OK." As if I have a choice.

I look at the Way-Back and recognize my old high school. I know precisely where we are and what's about to take place. I let out another deep sigh, and my hands coil into clenched fists under the table.

I'm getting an aerial view of the proceedings. This is what I see: There are two intersecting corridors lined with lockers in my high school. The corridors are at right angles to each other, so if you're walking down one corridor, you can't see what's coming from the other until they intersect.

Down one hallway comes Wayne Asbury. He's got his books tucked under one arm, a pencil behind one ear, his shirt tail hanging out the back of his pants, one shoelace untied, and a smear of jelly over his right cheek from lunch. His glasses are on crooked, and he's pretending that he's driving a car, shifting gears in the air and walking faster down the hallway with each motion of his right hand. The short story is this: Wayne is a slob and has been ever since I met him in ninth grade. He is bullied constantly and always picked on by the "hard guys," the jocks who are stronger than Wayne.

Down the other hallway—unbeknownst to Wayne—are two of the hard guys. I know them and avoid them whenever possible, though they have never picked on me. I never went out for sports except for track and field, cross-country running. But I worked out in the school gym almost daily, and the gym instructor had taken a liking to me, so he taught me how to box—how to fight. The workouts had paid off; as a senior, I was the third strongest boy in my class.

Wayne is approaching the intersection, and so are the two hard guys.

At this point I see myself emerge from one of the classrooms Wayne has just passed. I know it's after school, and I have just finished an extra assignment with my math teacher, so I'm minding my own business.

I shoot a glance over to Mr. O, who directs my attention back to the scene unfolding before me.

Wayne has reached the intersection at precisely the same time as the two jocks.

"Well, look what we have here, Shotgun."

Shotgun was the nickname of one of the bullies.

"Yeah." He snickered. "This is gonna be fun."

Meanwhile, Wayne adjusts his glasses, drops one of his books, and looks around to see whether he can somehow escape.

"Hey, Wayne," Shotgun calls out as he approaches his victim. "Did you put your jock strap on backward again?"

"Yeah, Wayne, did you put it on backward?" Dale, the other hard guy, taunts. They both laugh like someone who enjoys intimidating others.

I watch Wayne as he nervously takes a step back.

Dale walks over to where a trash can has been placed, picks it up, and dumps all the trash on the floor. He looks at Wayne as he reveals his idea. "Hey, Shotgun, I think Wayne needs to pick up the trash. Oh, better yet, maybe we should put him *in* the trash can!"

They cackle.

Shotgun steps closer to Wayne, and before Wayne has any chance to react, he's flicked Wayne's glasses off his head.

Dale runs up and gets on one side of Wayne while Shotgun gets on the other.

Shotgun yells, "On three!"

"Three!" Dale barks.

They pick Wayne up and walk over to the trash can, where they toss him in headfirst.

Wayne is thrashing about, trying to get out, but it's no use because they're both holding him down.

At this point I see myself running toward the scene. I've dropped my books, and the look on my face is grim. It's two against one, but I don't care—there's no hesitation. Before Shotgun and Dale can do anything, I hit them both with a flying tackle. The trash can crashes to the floor, and Wayne tumbles out.

Shotgun is slammed against one of the lockers while Dale is sliding across the floor.

Without pause I leap toward Shotgun. I smash my fist into his face, cut his upper lip, and knock his nose into next week.

Grabbing his hair, I slam his head against the locker, and Shotgun slumps to the floor, unconscious.

I see my high school self turn to Dale, who is crawling backward. Finally, he springs to his feet and runs away.

"Chicken!" I shout after him as I turn to see how Wayne is doing. I go over and pick up Wayne's books and find his glasses.

At this point all the commotion has raised a red flag, and two teachers are running down the hall toward us. I recognize one of them as the assistant principal, Mr. Marshall, who has a vendetta against me.

"Frisbee!" he yells. "I saw the whole thing. You're in big trouble, mister."

At this point Mr. O pauses the Way-Back. "You really were angry, weren't you?"

"More like enraged."

"Rightfully so. You came to Wayne's defense. He was essentially defenseless, and it was two against one. Not fair at all."

"I know what happens next. Do you want to skip to the chase?" I ask.

"Yes and no. How about I go through the events with the Way-Back, and we go from there. But let's talk about Wayne."

"OK."

"He was a friend. Even though you were also embarrassed by him, you liked him and helped him out whenever you could."

I nod silently.

"Why were you his friend?" Mr. O folds his hands in front of him.

I think back so many years ago—back to ninth grade—and then I reply, "Here's the first time I met Wayne. It was our freshman year, and he was sitting across the aisle from me. We had our new English books, and everyone in the class used to cover them with brown paper bags. I heard Wayne go *psst* to get my attention. I look across the aisle. He's holding up his English book that he's covered with a supermarket brown paper bag, except he's drawn a new cover. It's very elaborate, and it says, '*How to Speak English GOODER.*' I take one look at it and burst out laughing. I have to stifle my laughter; otherwise I'll get kicked out of class."

"That's pretty good. I mean gooder!" Mr. O chortles. "Actually, *gooder* and *worser* should be accepted as legitimate vocabulary words. I'll have to look into that. But please, continue."

"You have to understand"—I smile at the thought—"that when Wayne laughed, his entire body would shake, and his face would go completely red. He was in his element. He loved to make people laugh, and I was a good candidate. He had a great sense of humor, and he made me laugh all throughout that year.

"Another time, I heard the all-too-familiar *psst.* I looked across the aisle, and he had taken his fist and made a face by tucking his thumb into the other four fingers, then drawing two eyes above and inking in the lips. Then he would whisper, 'Hey, Bob!' moving his thumb, which was his newly created puppet's mouth. I almost got kicked out of class because I was laughing so hard."

"So even though Wayne was an outcast, you liked him, befriended him, and helped him whenever you could. Is that right?"

I nod. "That's why I went ballistic when Shotgun and Dale stuffed him headfirst into the trash can. I don't regret what I did."

"Then the assistant principal, Mr. Marshall, suspends you."

"Yeah, Shotgun had a mild concussion and a nasty cut on his upper lip. I was labeled the instigator, even though Wayne came to my rescue and told the truth about what had happened. It didn't matter. Mr. Marshall had it out for me and suspended me, and I wasn't allowed to graduate with my class. I turned eighteen that year, so I enlisted in the Air Force, and the rest is history."

"You found yourself in flight school and graduated at the top of your class," Mr. O points out. "You became a pilot and then flew F-16s. After that, you flew commercially—for the rest of your life—eventually becoming captain."

"Yeah, that's about it."

"So you can see how good came out of something meant to do you harm. Mr. Marshall was wrong in his actions; they were biased. But they set you on a course that would eventually become your path through life, and you excelled at it. Not everyone is so fortunate."

"I know where you're going with this. I need to forgive all of it. Mr. Marshall, Shotgun, Dale, and even Wayne."

Mr. O clears his throat. "You forgot your parents. You were bitter toward them because they didn't come to your rescue—they didn't defend you against Mr. Marshall."

"Yeah, that's when I left home and never returned. You know about all this. My parents never taught me anything, and this was the last straw. They sided with Mr. Marshall. I never had their support—never."

"We haven't talked about your mother yet, so it's good that you're bringing her into the mix." Mr. O opens my file and sorts through some pages. "Uh, here it is. We should get into this at some point; you do carry a lot of bitterness toward her."

"You're right, and we never reconciled. I can't even recall a conversation we had while she was alive. It's just not there. She never came to anything I ever did. She was absent from my life. Essentially, from what I know now, she was unfit to be a mother."

"You were the only child."

"Yeah, you would have thought there'd be some kind of connection, but looking back, I have come to realize that I was rejected from the womb. She passed away while I was in the Air Force. I went to the funeral, but I didn't cry—I felt nothing. It didn't matter. She was my mother, but she was never my *mother.*" I use my hands to illustrate air quotes. "Really, she was unfit to be a mother." I slump down in my chair.

Mr. O sighs as he explains, "Bob, life is like putting the pieces of a puzzle together. Each person's puzzle is unique, and only they can assemble it. Some people assemble it early—some later in life. Some remain fractured and never put their puzzle together. They never learn who they are. Your mother was one of those people who never put her puzzle together. She was stuck."

"I've never heard it put that way, *stuck*. You're right. She was stuck. Something happened to her along the way that ruined her life—even with my dad. He told me once that Mom was a very closed-up person—a cold fish, as they say. Their initial romance produced me, but after that she always found an excuse not to be intimate with him. They wound up sleeping in different bedrooms. I never thought much of it until I realized that this wasn't normal. Mind you, I didn't know what so-called *normal* was until I met Evelyn. There was real love in her family of siblings and parents; that was foreign to me. But it was Evelyn who taught me what love is. Evelyn and my best friend, Fred."

The thought comes to me, and I press my lips tightly together, tension spreading throughout my body. "Is she here?"

Mr. O's face is very serious—the most serious I have ever seen it. He slowly shakes his head. "No, Bob, she's not here."

I think, "Wait…what?" I'm not sure how to deal with what Mr. O just told me.

"Not everyone makes it," he says gently. "Remember, it's free will."

Part of me wants to cry—part of me wishes there was something I could do. "There's nothing anyone can do…is there?"

Mr. O shakes his head again and then points to the Way-Back. "You know what you have to do. I'll leave you again so you can have your privacy."

With that Mr. O quietly leaves, and I am left looking at the scene frozen in time on the Way-Back. At least Wayne is no longer in the trash can. I look at my wheel, close my eyes, and do the work. But I can't stop wondering what happened to my mother that she didn't "make it."

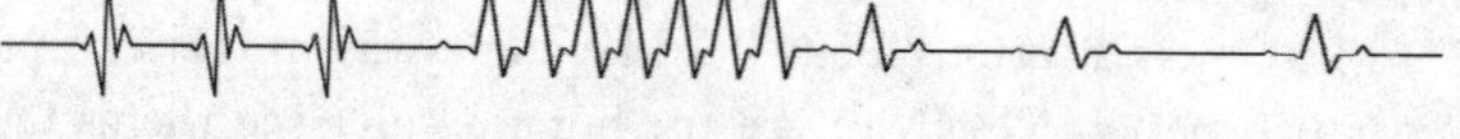

# 21
# THE CHEERING SECTION

R. O IS back in the Waiting Room. He pats the file and smiles. "You're doing great, Bob. Keep doing what you're doing. You're on the right track. You're doing the right thing. We're closing in on it now."

Again, I hear applause coming from somewhere outside the Waiting Room, so I ask, "Where is that applause coming from?"

"Do you want to see it?"

"See what?"

"Your cheering section."

"*My* cheering section? That's where the applause is coming from? Seriously?"

"Of course! There are a lot of folks out there who are watching the proceedings and rooting for you. They don't get all the *private* information; that's just between you and me. But when they see one of the spokes go from dark to light, they get excited and cheer you on."

"I don't believe it! Are you serious?"

"Remember, they have all the time in the world. Well, I should say in *eternity*." He laughs. "The most important part is that these people love you."

I'm taken aback by this. Who are "these people" that Mr. O

is talking about? I'm not sure I want to find out. But then again, if they're rooting for me, it has to be a good thing, right?

Another thing comes to my mind, so I ask, "How do they see into the Waiting Room?"

Mr. O gets a serious look. "It's like a one-way mirror except so much better. They can see us, but we can't see them. Of course, I can change that so we can see them if you want to. I can introduce some of the people in the stands."

"Stands? There are *stands*? Like…like bleachers?" I'm flabbergasted by this.

"Oh yes, there are quite a lot of folks out there."

"How long have these 'folks' been in the stands?"

"Since before you arrived."

I'm frowning at Mr. O, trying to get my head around what he's saying. Who are these people? "Since before I arrived? You mean they *knew* I was coming here…to the Waiting Room?"

"Of course. There's always a welcoming committee."

"But I didn't get a welcoming committee. I wound up here in the Waiting Room."

"True, but the welcoming committee was here just the same, and you've heard them applauding your efforts."

"I can see them? Who…who are they?" Is there a noise in the Waiting Room, or are my ears ringing?

"I can show you if you're ready. How do you want to start? From the beginning…well, we can't do that. It would take too long…"

"The beginning of what? I don't understand."

"Bob, everyone is connected. Are you aware that even scientists on earth talk about a common maternal ancestor from which all other human beings came?"

I nod, bewildered. I've heard about this but never really thought about it.

"We can't go all the way back, but I can show you some of

the people you know who have gotten here before you. And some of the people that you've never heard of."

"People I've never heard of?"

"Exactly. How far back have you traced your family line?"

I think about this for a minute. "I heard about one of my great-grandfathers, but he passed away before I was born, so I never knew him."

Mr. O leans back in his chair. "Do you know what one of my favorite things to do here is?"

"I have no idea."

"It's to introduce a new arrival to their family line. It's always great to watch their faces light up as we go back through the centuries."

"Centuries? How is that possible?"

"Well, some families keep records, but they only go back so far, and then the trail gets hard to follow. But our records here are impeccable. Why don't I show you what I'm talking about?"

Before I can respond, Mr. O has done something, and one of the walls in the Waiting Room has opened, revealing a set of bleachers. There are perhaps a few hundred people in the stands. Some of them are holding flags with my picture on them, while others have hand-painted signs saying things such as "*Go, Bob!*" I am literally flabbergasted. Then I recognize one of my uncles, but he looks really young, vibrant, and full of life—not the sickly, broken-down man that I remember. His nickname was Timer because when he was born, his face was all wrinkled, so my grandfather called him the *Old Timer*, and the name stuck.

"Hi, Bob!" I hear him yell from the bleachers. "You're doing great! Keep doing what you're doing!"

Uncle Timer turns, and there's a man next to him I don't recognize. I turn to Mr. O and ask, "Who's the man next to Uncle Timer?"

"Ah, you don't recognize him, do you?"

"No, I don't."

"That's your grandfather." Mr. O clearly enjoys this.

"But…"

"I know," he says, reading my thoughts again. "Everyone here is young, vibrant—whole, hale, and hearty, as I like to say."

"But how?"

"Well, everyone is changed *in a twinkling of an eye.* They are made new when they receive eternal life. It's complicated, but you can see with your own eyes that this is the case."

I look at my grandfather and his son, my Uncle Timer. They wave at me, and my uncle holds up his sign: "*Go, Bob!*"

As I stare in disbelief, Mr. O continues, "Let me explain it this way. Human beings are robbed because of the sin and death that came into the world by the Dragon, who, by the way, only exists to rob, kill, and destroy."

"How are we robbed?" I ask.

"Do you know who your great, great-grandfather is?"

I think for a moment and shake my head. "No."

"Precisely! This is part of what entered the world so long ago but will be righted—eventually. You were robbed of knowing your great, great-grandfather, but think of this: Did your great, great-grandfather know his great, great-grandfather?" Mr. O shakes his head. "He was robbed of knowing him, just as you were, and back and back it goes—all the way to Adam."

"To Adam, as in *the* Adam—and Eve?"

"Exactly, that's where everything that was put in place *and was very good* was corrupted by the Dragon. Can you imagine the *big* family reunion once we get everything sorted out?"

"What do you mean by 'sorted out'?"

"Well, that's a three-hour discussion. But briefly put, once we get to the thousand-year reign of Jesus from Jerusalem, things will change drastically. You will meet with your ancestors, dance with them, celebrate with them—and remember, you have all the time you need to get to know one another."

I'm looking at these people—my ancestors in the stands. Some of them are dressed in clothing from different periods of history. "Why are some people in costumes?"

Mr. O chuckles. "They're not dressed in costumes; those clothes are what they wore when they were alive on earth. Some people feel more comfortable in their 'period' clothes, while others love the linen clothes that are created here, which they have the option to wear."

I look up at the stands again and notice a man in what looks like a costume that a Crusader would have worn a thousand years ago. He's holding a "*Go, Bob!*" sign in one hand, and in the other he's brandishing a beautiful sword lifted high above his head.

"I'm related to him?" I ask in disbelief.

Mr. O nods. "You certainly are. That's Balian of Ibelin. He was a key figure in the defense of Jerusalem a thousand years before you were born."

"You have got to be kidding me. I'm related to a Crusader?"

"Like I told you, everyone is robbed of seeing where they come from and who they are related to—all the family connections. We fix all that here. And it's almost too much for some people to handle because they are filled with so much wonder, joy, and awe. We make everything new here."

I mumble, thinking out loud, "I'm related to a Crusader?"

Mr. O waves to the Crusader, and I hear him shout out, "Hail to the King!"

I ask, "Who's the King he's talking about?"

"All in good time, all in good time," Mr. O says with a smile.

I hear someone yelling from the cheering section, "Bob! Go, Bob! You're on the right track! Go, Bob!"

It's a woman dressed in what looks like a beautiful dress, but it's unlike anything I've ever seen before. It's shimmering and seems to accentuate her body. Her long, brown hair reaches to her waist, and she appears so full of love and energy. I ask, "Who is that?"

"That's your great, great, great-grandmother. She was alive during the Civil War. Amazing, isn't it?"

"I had no idea."

"See how the entire human race has no idea of its origins and how everyone is connected in some way?"

"Does everyone look young here?"

"Yes. Everyone looks like they are in the prime of life here. No one ages, and no one grows old. There is no sickness, infirmity, or death. Everyone here has eternal life. Everyone is whole, hale, and hearty."

"I never knew about this woman. Unbelievable."

"You see, once again, how everyone has been robbed—their identities, in many ways, stolen from them."

I nod. As Mr. O said, it's almost too much to take in. I look over at the crowd in the stand—my cheering section. Then I see a familiar face: It's Tom Weller. He died in a car crash when he was only sixteen. We used to go fishing together. He was a good friend. He looks just like he did the last time I saw him. But then he suddenly matures into a man in his late twenties.

"Bob! Let's go fishing soon!" he says. He laughs as he holds up his sign that says, "*You've got this, Bob!*"

"That's Tom Weller! He's here!"

"Yes, he is, and so are a lot of other people you know. Some you don't know, like your great, great, great-grandmother from the Civil War. Do you want to meet someone from *waaaay* back?" Mr. O laughs.

"Sure!"

"Here you go. Look in the back row of the stands."

I look over the bleachers and spot a man clothed in what appear to be animal skins. "Who is he?" I ask.

"He's a distant relative who was a shepherd. He lived in what is now Portugal. He lived a good, long life. And even though he couldn't read, he listened to the good news that was brought to him by traveling preachers."

"What year was this? How far back?"

"Around the fifth century."

I'm astonished by Mr. O's nonchalant answer.

"How can you possibly keep track of all this?" I ask.

"Don't sweat the details; just enjoy what you're seeing and realize that these are your relatives—where you come from."

I look again at all the people in the stands with different costumes, and as I do, the view begins to fade. Just before it does, all the people unite in one last cheer together. "You're doing the right thing! Keep doing what you're doing! You're on the right track!" With that the cheering section disappears, but I hear one last cry in unison: "Go, Bob!"

The wheel appears, and Mr. O is looking at one of the remaining dark spokes. I recognize the person at the end immediately: It's my daughter, Marsha.

"I was waiting for this," I say as I stare at the picture. "I knew you would bring it up eventually, and now here it is."

Mr. O nods. "Yes, let's talk about Marsha."

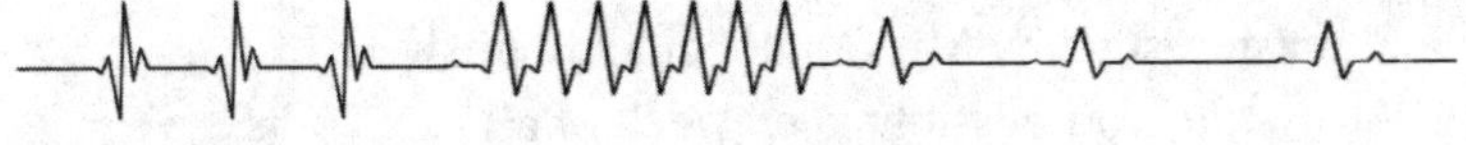

# 22
# SPIRIT OF BAPHOMET

"WHERE SHALL WE start with Marsha?" Mr. O asks.

I hang my head and let out a doleful sigh. "She broke her mother's heart—mine too. And it got to the point where I never wanted to see her again."

Mr. O is listening intently and wearing an empathetic expression.

I continue, "She was a wonderful little girl and then an inquisitive teenager, always exploring anything she was interested in. Never caused us an ounce of trouble. Straight A student. She would light up a room with her enthusiasm for life. In her senior year, she applied for college and was accepted. That's where all the trouble began. She had dated through high school but was never serious about anyone, and then this idiot she met at college her freshman year—who, by the way, was three years older than Marsha—ruined her."

"Go on."

"He would hit her and verbally abuse her, making fun of the way she looked. She didn't know how to handle it and didn't tell us anything until she finally had enough and broke it off. But by then the damage was done. She moved into an apartment we paid for to get her away from all the drama. Then she met a woman across the hallway who was a student as well—and a full-blown lesbian. Marsha had never met a lesbian until she went to college, and she befriended this woman. Eileen, that's her name, but she changed it to Jake when she came out as gay. She was in the process of transitioning to a man, and she looked more like a man than a woman."

I took a heavy breath and let out a labored sigh before I continued.

"She *groomed* Marsha. Remember, Marsha was alone and hurting from the breakup with her abusive boyfriend, but she had no idea what Eileen was doing. It was subtle, and I think drugs were involved—mostly pot, but they were still drugs. Then Eileen made her move, and the rest is history."

"I'm sorry that happened," Mr. O says.

"Eileen had a coming-out party for Marsha," I recalled, "and a few other gay women came over to Eileen's apartment. Marsha had beautiful blonde hair that reached almost to her waist. So at the coming-out party, they cut off all her hair. Someone took a video of it. A few women took turns chopping off locks of her hair while the rest cheered. Lock after lock fell to the floor. Marsha cheered as well and, at one point, took the scissors and cut a lock of her hair that Eileen held for her. Then, to our horror, they kissed. After this, an older woman with a crewcut took clippers and buzzed Marsha's head. When she was finished, Marsha looked almost bald. When my wife saw the video, she couldn't stop crying—and that was the beginning of the end for me. It went downhill from there."

I exhale and glance over at Marsha's picture on the wheel. It's still dark, as I knew it would be.

Mr. O looks saddened by what I have told him. He takes off his glasses, and it looks like he's wiping tears from his eyes. The room is very quiet.

He says, softly, "A woman's hair is her crowning glory."

I've never heard this before, so I repeat, "Crowning glory?"

"Yes, that's the way she was created. As you know, a woman is different from a man. She was taken from Adam's side—from his rib—a bit of genetic engineering if you will. Until Eve was created, there had never been a female human being."

"I never thought of it like that. So Eve was the first woman… ever?"

Mr. O chuckles and puts his glasses back on. "Yes, she was, and this is what got the fallen angels in trouble. They had already left their first estate in heaven well before the creation of Eve, and later, when they saw that the daughters of men were beautiful…well, that's when the abominations started."

"They seduced women, right?"

"Yes. They *took wives of whomever they wished,* and this was part of the Dragon's plan—his plan to corrupt the image of what the Lord God had created, to create a hybrid being that was never supposed to be. As I told you before, the fallen angels had sex with human women and created a hybrid being. These beings are called Nephilim, and they are soulless."

"I still don't understand why I never heard about this before."

"I know; most pastors are ignorant of this. Let me tell you something: This is the key to the entire *Guidebook to the Supernatural.*"

"That's what you call the Bible, right?"

"Yes, and I'm fond of calling it that because that's what it is, a guidebook. Nowhere is this more graphically demonstrated than when the fallen angels took wives and had children by them. The progeny of this unholy union was the Nephilim, and all this resulted in a forty-day deluge known as the flood of Noah."

"Yeah, if it really happened," I interject.

"Bob, it did happen," Mr. O says. "Are you aware that almost every culture on earth has a flood story? All this goes back to the mixing of the seed, or what I call the *seed war.* As I said earlier, if you understand *this* passage, the rest of the *Guidebook* opens up. Here it is. *The offspring of the Dragon will be at war with the offspring of the woman. He shall crush your head and you will bruise his heel.*[1] That's it! That's the whole megillah, as they say."

I'm pondering what Mr. O has just explained. It's hard to comprehend. "So it's a seed war. But I thought angels couldn't reproduce?"

"Trust me, that's not the case."

"What does this have to do with Marsha?"

"The Dragon's corruption knows no bounds. Look at all the confusion going on, even as we speak right now. Men trying to be women, and women trying to be men. Of course, that's impossible, no matter what a person tries to do. Marsha was lied to, and she bought the lie. She abandoned her crowning glory and cut off her hair to become something that will never work—ever."

My mournful sigh is the only sound in the beat of silence. "I don't know how to deal with this. I never thought she would be involved in this."

"I know," Mr. O says. "People don't just wake up on a Monday morning and say, 'Gee, I think I'll try to become something I'm not.' It doesn't work that way. The Dragon and his cohorts lead them slowly and very methodically down a path of destruction, and after a time, what was unthinkable to that person becomes their reality. They actually embrace it. It is deception on a grand scale."

"Marsha isn't Marsha anymore. She's turned into someone I no longer recognize—or can even relate to. It's devastating."

"Bob, I call this the *spirit of the age,* and it has a name."

"A name? What, the gay agenda has a name?"

"Specifically, what happened to Marsha and countless others is the *spirit of Baphomet*. Have you ever heard of this?"

"No."

"Most people haven't. You lived in a supernatural world

while you were on earth; although unseen, it is just behind the veil. However, the veil is thinning, and forces that most people are unaware of are working to bring people to destruction."

"Who…what is Baphomet?"

Mr. O lets out a deep sigh. He goes to the Way-Back, and I see a figure seated on a throne. It has the head of a goat, the body of a man, and the breasts of a woman. In short, it is a monstrosity.

"This is Baphomet; he is the spirit of the age you live in. He is a chimera—part man, part woman, and part animal—just as in the days of Noah."

I stare at the picture in disbelief.

"Right out of the pit of hell," he says, soberly. "Only a few years ago, what you call 'transgenderism' was unheard of; now it is almost a status symbol to have a child who is in transition."

"Mr. O, my wife and I went to a support group when Marsha came out. We couldn't deal with any of this. The last straw for me was when Marsha told us she wanted to get her breasts removed."

"Yes, and young men are castrated and pumped with female hormones. But let's get to the root here. While I understand that you are distancing yourself from Marsha, she is your daughter, and you have to forgive her. That doesn't mean you have to condone the lifestyle she has chosen, but you have to love her and forgive her—and Eileen too. Notice that I refuse to call Eileen 'Jake,' because she will never be a man, no matter how many hormone shots she takes. This is the lie—that somehow, with enough hormones and switching body parts around, one can become what they are not. Their DNA will always, and I mean always, reflect who they really are."

"I don't know where to begin with this," I say, searching. "Marsha is a completely different person than the one we raised, and I don't know how to even relate to her."

"You don't have to relate to her; you're here now. But you do need to light up the spoke, forgive her, and bless her—as well as Eileen and the ex-boyfriend who were the root of all this."

My shoulders sag, and I hang my head. "I feel like we failed her in some way."

"It wasn't your fault. Remember, people have free will. Also, what Marsha endured from her so-called boyfriend impacted her in ways that shaped her future. As I stated before, some people never heal from their brokenness. They remain fractured all their lives. However, if they turn to me, I can heal them. Some do, but most do not, so they carry their brokenness with them and embrace it. Think about this, though: Where there is breath and life, there is hope."

"Hope? For Marsha?"

Mr. O nods and smiles encouragingly. "Yes, and even for Eileen. People can change, and many do."

Though I don't really understand the depth of what Mr. O is saying, I manage to say, "I know what to do, but I want to be alone again."

Mr. O slowly gets up from his chair and leaves the Waiting Room.

I'm alone, and it's very quiet. I look over at the spoke. I shake my head. I don't know how to make any of this right, but I have learned that forgiveness is the key to it all. I also know I can't fake this. I'm breathing heavily; a part of me can't do this. But then I reflect on what the Escape Tunnel was like and my Aunt Mary. I don't want to go there. I have a choice, and I know in the depths of my soul that I will make the right one. Still, it's heartbreaking.

I take a deep breath and do what I have learned while here in the Waiting Room: I forgive and bless. Amidst it all, I sense a ray of hope, and I look over at the wheel to find that Marsha's spoke has lit up.

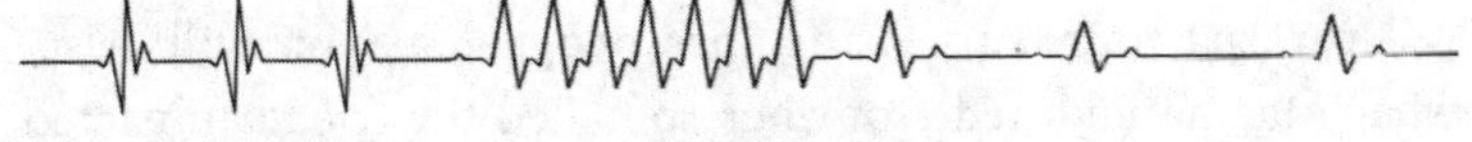

# 23

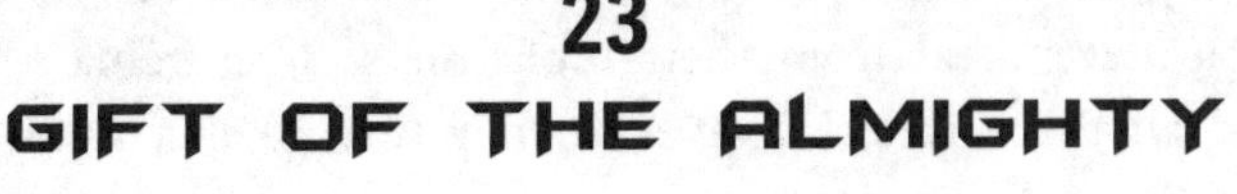


Mr. O bursts into the room. "Let's go, quick! It's about to start at any moment."

I rise from my chair. "What's about to start? Where are we going?" Apparently, I'm not moving fast enough.

"I'll explain on the way. You'll love this." Mr. O grabs my arm and hurries me toward the door.

"I lit up Marsha's spoke," I tell him.

Mr. O pauses for only a second in the doorway, looking at me. "You're doing the right thing. Good for you! But we have to hurry. There's standing room only for this."

I have no idea what Mr. O is talking about, but before we leave, I hear my cheering section applauding and whooping it up just outside the Waiting Room.

For the first time, I'm going through the same door that Mr. O emerged from when I came here. I am dumbfounded as I see a long hallway that stretches far out into the distance; it looks like it goes on forever. On either side are doors: Some of them are plain, while others are very ornate. Some are hand-carved, while others are wrought iron with intricate workings. Some have mother-of-pearl inlay, others look like they are made from ancient timbers, and still others are made of something I can only describe as shimmering glass. I want to stop and look at each one, but Mr. O has me by the arm, and we are running down the hallway. Mr. O is pretty spry, and it's all I can do to keep up with him.

"Here it is," he says. Without waiting, knocking, or catching his breath, he bursts into a large theater. We're high up in the balcony, looking down at the stage below us, where an exquisite grand piano is polished to perfection. "Quick! He's about to start!"

"Who's about to—"

"Shhhh," Mr. O cuts me off, whispering. "You'll see in a moment. Notice the place is packed. It's always this way. He really draws a crowd up here."

"Who?"

"Shhh. Just watch."

The lights suddenly dim, and the audience settles in. It's somewhat of an intimate venue, as I would estimate it holds no more than five hundred people. Every seat is taken. We are in a private booth up in the balcony. From here I have a bird's-eye view to watch whatever is about to happen, which I presume is a piano recital. Mr. O is leaning forward expectantly in his chair. From the side of the stage, a figure appears.

"There he is!" Mr. O exclaims.

I see a man of medium height with wild, brown hair, a high forehead, and a serious expression. He waves to the crowd as he enters, and then looks up and, to my amazement, waves to Mr. O, who waves back.

"Who is it?" I think out loud, still having no idea who I'm looking at.

The audience turns to see who the figure on stage is waving at, and a collective gasp goes up, followed by a thunderous call of "Hail to the King!"

Mr. O waves to the crowd, and after a few moments, everyone settles in their chairs again.

"Why do people keep saying, 'Hail to the King'?" I ask.

"I'll explain all in good time. There she is!" Mr. O points to the crowd below.

"Who?"

"It's Elise. She always sits in the front row—always. She never misses a concert. They're very close, you see."

The pianist has settled on the piano bench.

"Please tell me who this is; I have no idea," I say, revealing my frustration.

Mr. O leans closer and whispers, "It's Beethoven."

"Beethoven?" I say a bit too loudly before getting back to an appropriate whisper. "Seriously?" I'm more than a little surprised.

"Yes! Isn't this great? He's going to play one of my favorite compositions, the *Pathetique*. It's very virtuosic. You'll love it."

I nod dumbly—not sure whether I've ever heard the piece of music Mr. O is referring to.

The audience is still, almost reverent.

I watch as Beethoven sits motionless in front of the keyboard. He's almost trancelike, I imagine, because he's concentrating deeply on what he's about to perform. And then his hands hit the keys in a thunderous chord. I am taken aback by the unexpected intensity of it. I glance at Mr. O; his eyes are closed as he relishes every moment.

Beethoven continues, and I become wrapped up in the moment—in the intensity of chord progressions, the intricate cascading notes, the rumbling bass notes, and the emotion being stirred within me—as I listen intently. I feel my soul being absorbed in every note, and even though the music is very complex, it is accessible. Themes repeat. Beethoven's fingers are flying across the keys softly and then suddenly striking with such force that I wonder if he's going to damage the piano! I am swept away in the moment. He is a musical genius.

The piece ends, and Elise is the first person to jump to

her feet with a standing ovation, but the rest of the crowd follows quickly.

Mr. O is already on his feet, and I follow suit, joining in the thunderous applause. Beethoven rises from the bench and takes several long, protracted bows in appreciation.

"We have to go," Mr. O says. Before I can say or do anything, he's grabbed my arm again. Out the door we go, and then we are back in the endless hallway.

"He really is a genius," he says. "What a gift."

I nod, not knowing what to say.

"Well, here we are," Mr. O says as we reach what I assume is the door to the Waiting Room. But as he opens it, it's not the Waiting Room—we're standing on the Giza Plateau in Egypt before the Great Pyramid of Giza!

"How is this...?" I stammer.

"Sorry, wrong door." Mr. O chuckles as he closes the door and moves further down the hallway. "I love doing that to the folks who come here. Everyone has the same response."

Mr. O opens another door, and I cautiously peer inside, but I can see this is the Waiting Room, so I step in. The familiar wheel is there by the table, and it's mostly lit up. We take our seats across from each other.

Mr. O looks at me and says, "Let's talk about your son, Phil."

I nod, knowing where this is going. So I begin, saying, "I wasn't there for him when he needed me. I was flying a lot back then. Sometimes days would go by before I would get home again, especially flying to Australia and back. Phil was a senior in high school at that point, and I missed most of his senior year, including his graduation. Then he went off to college, and that was it. He hardly ever came home, and when he did, he was distant. We had nothing in common and nothing to talk about."

"Yes, but something happened that *stuck in your craw*, as they say."

I let out another sigh. "Yes. He found a mentor in one of the teachers at college, and he connected with him. His name was Cliff. They would play racquetball and go on ski trips together. Cliff taught him how to drink whiskey, and he was the one who introduced him to his first real girlfriend, Janie. But Cliff was an atheist, and before we knew it, Phil had abandoned his faith and become agnostic. Not that he was a Jesus freak or anything before college, but at one time he did believe, and that was the issue—especially for Evelyn."

I pause for a moment to collect my thoughts. "When he came home for the holidays, he was distant and closed up. We never really had a conversation after that. Then he and Janie got serious, and they moved in together—something Evelyn and I disapproved of. In the end he drifted away from the family, and the only time we saw him was at Christmas. Eventually it was only for Christmas Day. After he graduated, he and Janie broke up. He continued to drift further away from us to the point where sometimes we don't hear from him for months, even though we leave messages on his phone. He just completely disconnected."

Mr. O grows more serious. "What about the abortion?"

"That was the final straw for both Evelyn and me. The abortion is what caused Phil and Janie to break up. I'm not sure of the whole story, but Evelyn did talk to Janie a year or so later when she ran into her at the grocery store. This is all I know. Janie got pregnant and wanted to keep the baby and get married. Phil would have none of it and forced her to get an abortion. It was around six months into her pregnancy that she did it—but only because Phil insisted. Shortly afterward, Janie left him. Evelyn was so angry that the next time she saw Phil, she slapped him in the face without warning. Phil didn't know what he had been slapped for, but Evelyn gave him a piece of her mind and made it really clear that she felt robbed of what would have been her grandbaby. After that, everything fell apart between Phil and the family—everything."

Mr. O says, "The baby is here."

I gasp, stunned. "Here? How can that be?"

"Contrary to what many people believe, life begins at the moment of conception. This is when El Shaddai bestows the soul upon this new creation."

"Who is El Shaddai?"

"Sorry. El Shaddai is God Almighty. Only He can give a soul, and it is He who bestows the soul into that tiny seed, which will become a human being—given time, of course."

"So the little one who was aborted is here?"

Mr. O nods gravely. "Yes, he is."

I think about this and then blurt out, "There have been millions of abortions since it became legal. All of them are here?"

"They're here. We have a special place for them."

Suddenly I feel overwhelmed, and I burst out crying.

"You feel the weight of it, don't you?" Mr. O asks softly.

I nod with my face in my hands.

"What is happening to you is a gift," he says. "I'm letting you feel some of the weight of the murder, the death, and the souls who were ripped from what should've been the safest place for them: their mother's womb. I'm letting you hear their silent screams."

I am frozen in place as Mr. O is talking, and I can't put into words what he has allowed me to experience.

He continues, "Now all these little ones are here, and they are safe and whole. As I said, we have a special place for them. Their lives were taken from them, but here all is made right, made new, made whole."

"If people only knew what you just showed me and what you let me experience…the weight of it…they would change."

Mr. O nods. "Life is precious, fragile, and a gift from the Almighty. It was He who created all life and set the universe in motion. He spoke it into existence."

I gather myself together and sit up, wiping my eyes on the sleeve of my shirt.

"All this will change one day," he adds. "The time is coming for the King to return to earth and rule for a thousand years."

"Is it soon?"

"Yes, the King will return soon, and His feet will touch down on the Mount of Olives, which will split it in two. He will rule with a rod of iron. There will be no more abortions, human trafficking, crack houses, dope dens, homelessness, drunkards, and men will learn war no more. All the evil that has ruled men's hearts for thousands of years will be put down, as the King will rule."

Riveted by his description, I nearly whisper, "It's almost too good to be true."

Mr. O gives me one of those looks that makes me wish I hadn't commented.

"I can assure you, Bob, what was written will come to pass. What was foretold is unfolding."

I turn to the wheel and see that Phil's spoke is lit up. I'm amazed because I didn't do the work—at least not the way I have before. I suppose I forgave him without verbalizing it.

I'm startled by the sound of deafening applause outside the room.

# 24
# SHORTCUT

Mr. O is smiling and seems a little excited. "We have a way to take a shortcut for the next spoke. By the way, you're almost done. Look!"

I look at the wheel, and he is right, of course. The wheel is all lit up except for one last spoke. But I notice something I haven't seen before. "This last spoke looks different from all the others. Why is that?"

"I call this the *forget-about-its,*" he explains.

"Forget what?"

"Exactly."

"Exactly what?"

"You mean exactly *who,* not *what.*" Mr. O gives a hearty laugh.

"I have no idea who or what you're talking about!"

"Sorry, but I needed some relief from all this."

"You mean this weighs on you too?"

He takes a deep breath, followed by a sigh. "You have no idea how much this weighs on me. No matter. Back to the forget-about-its."

"Forget about what?"

"Not *what* but *who*." He starts laughing again. "OK, sorry. Let's get serious. I'll give you an example."

He waves his hand over the Way-Back, and I see my eighteen-year-old self in my car. I'm driving on a two-lane road doing the speed limit when some guy in a souped-up Mustang goes blowing past me. I respond immediately with the middle-finger salute.

"You have a record of that?" I'm beside myself, knowing I've had a great many less-than-flattering moments over the decades while driving. "This is going to take a long time, isn't it?" I ask nervously. "I could be here forever!"

"True," Mr. O says, still rather chipper. "We could spend an eon here. But these are called the *forget-about-its* because you've *forgotten* about these little minor peccadillos."

"Peccadillos?"

"You gave the driver the middle-finger salute, but then a few moments later you forgot about the whole thing. Nevertheless, it's in your file and on the Way-Back. Now here we are dealing with the forget-about-its."

"But I don't even know who the knucklehead in the Mustang was!"

"There you go, calling the driver a knucklehead. This is precisely what I'm pointing out. You didn't exactly bless him, did you?"

I'm shifting uncomfortably in my seat, trying to think of some way I can get out of this.

"You know, Bob, there are a lot of these."

I'm fidgeting, thinking, "No kidding!" But instead, I ask, "How many are we looking at?" I sink down in my chair, not really wanting to know.

Mr. O looks at the file and hits fast-forward on the Way-Back, so I see a blur of figures that stretches through all my years on earth.

"The exact number is..." Mr. O pauses. "Do you really want to know?"

My only response is to sink lower in my chair. With my eyes darting around the room, I'm thinking that I'll never get out of here.

Mr. O clears his throat. "Here you go. It starts at the age of reason, which is 13 years of age; that's when accountability really starts. You left earth when you were 60, so we take 13 years from 60, and we get 47 years of accountability. Then we multiply this by 365 days, and it brings us to 17,155 days. Here's where it gets interesting. It's not only while driving but also while playing sports; having an attitude toward someone in the market, at the gas station, and on television; and on and on and on it goes. Most people never think about it, but *we* do, and it's all in your file."

"So how many times?" I ask, still not really wanting to know the answer.

"Brace yourself. Are you ready?"

"No, I'm not ready for this. I can only imagine! If I had known about this, I would have behaved differently."

"Trust me, nothing would have changed," he says, flatly, looking at me over his glasses.

"OK then," I give in, unable to escape it. "So what's the total?" I brace myself for the worst.

"Exactly 85,775 times you essentially cursed someone, either out loud or in your mind."

"I'll never get out of here," I mumble. "Wait a minute," I protest. "How is it cursing someone? I'm not cursing anyone."

"The middle finger isn't cursing?" Mr. O looks at me directly. "How about all the name-calling?"

"Name-calling? I didn't do that. I didn't call anyone names!"

Mr. O goes over the file and pulls out a few pages. He looks down his nose at me as he begins, "Here are just some of them: idiot, numbskull, moron, ape-man, Neanderthal, cretin, fool, nitwit, fetus brain, blockhead, bonehead, dimwit, dork, dumbbell, ignoramus, nincompoop, pinhead, imbecile, jerk, tomfool, donkey head, maniac..."

I look anywhere but at Mr. O.

"Shall I continue?" he asks.

"OK, I get the point. But these aren't curses, they're just... just..."

Mr. O cuts me off. "Well, they're not blessings, now, are they?"

"Well, maybe not blessings, exactly. They're just ways..." I'm really trying to grab on to something—anything—for defense.

"Bob," he says, fully aware of the ridiculousness of my avoidance, "answer my question, please. These are *not* blessings, are they?"

Still slumped in my chair, I twist a little to the left, wishing I could go through the floor. With nowhere to go, I finally answer with a low grumble, "No."

"That's the right answer. They're not blessings. And if they're not blessings, then what are they?"

"They're just words...just a way to blow off steam."

"Wrong answer." Mr. O taps down on a buzzer that appears on the table, and the room is filled with the obnoxious sound.

"OK, OK. But a *curse*? Seriously?"

"Yes, a curse. Everything people say has weight, whether good or bad. This is why blessing everyone, no matter what they do, is essential. Don't you remember reading in the *Guidebook to the Supernatural*, '*Bless those who persecute you*'?[1] It doesn't say poke them in the eye, now, does it? Or call them a derogatory name?"

I guiltily shake my head.

"Most people never learn to harness their tongue, to tame it. So they blurt out curses, just as you did while you were alive on earth—around 85,000 times."

"I didn't realize," I groan in surrender.

"Most people don't think about it, but the *Guidebook* instructs us to keep every thought accountable—and every thought means just that—*every* thought."

Overwhelmed by a feeling of contrition, I ask, "So how can I possibly light up this last spoke? I have 85,000 people to bless!"

"Well, the good news is, we can speed up the whole process with the Way-Back. We can do it at a very fast pace—more than you can grasp with your mind. I'll show you." Mr. O reaches under the table and comes up with a helmet.

I look at the strange contraption. "What's that?"

"I call it the accelerator."

"The what?"

This helmet reminds me of something from—what's the name of that movie? *Napoleon Dynamite!*—where Napoleon's brother, Kip, is wearing some goofy helmet. It looks like a tinfoil hat, only with something that looks like antennae sticking out of it.

"Once you put it on, you'll see how it works." With that Mr. O walks around to my side of the table and wiggles the helmet onto my head.

"I don't feel anything," I say, feeling utterly ridiculous.

"You will shortly. Oh wait, I forgot the special glasses."

He reaches under the table again and produces a pair of glasses with very thick lenses.

"Here, put these on," he says.

I look sideways at the strange spectacles as I obediently put them on, but I can't see a thing.

Mr. O goes to the Way-Back, and suddenly I see images of people I said nasty things to. While inside the helmet, I hear myself—dare I use Mr. O's words?—cursing them.

He says, "Now we're going to do this. Full speed ahead! Just brace yourself."

As I'm watching through the glasses, I see images flying by: slowly at first but then faster and faster. I hear my voice pronouncing curses on people, and with the increasing speed, they become like one long continuous sound, which is very unpleasant to my ears.

Faces, places, cars, buildings, friends, and people I've never met are blurring by faster and faster until they're almost indistinguishable. Yet somehow I can make out every instance, every person, every face.

At this point I can feel my body begin to vibrate in the chair.

"Steady, Bob!" Mr. O admonishes. "Hold the course!"

The images are flying by so fast they are almost imperceptible, yet I *still* can make out each individual instance.

Even faster now.

"Almost done, Bob! Hang in there!" Mr. O encourages me.

My entire body is vibrating. Images flash by faster than I can grasp them, and then suddenly there's nothing.

After a second, I ask, "That's it? Finished?"

"That's it! You're done. You took accountability and blessed everyone."

"I don't know how that's possible. All I heard was my…anger toward every person that flashed by."

"And you can't take any of that back, but what you did was take responsibility for your attitude, and now you can just bless everyone at the same time. Remember, Bob—blessings, not curses."

I nod, realizing my forehead is dripping beads of perspiration onto my shirt.

Mr. O gets up and removes the glasses and helmet. "How do you feel?"

I'm still processing what has happened. "Like I've been cleansed from something I didn't know was there. Like layers of dirt and filth have been lifted off me."

Mr. O nods with a knowing smile.

"So what happens now?"

"Hold your hand out to the spoke that's still dark and bless everyone there. Say that you're sorry for the cursing, that you take it all back, and that you bless everyone."

I look over at the wheel and see the dark spoke with faces flashing by at the end of it. I look once more at Mr. O.

He nods encouragingly. "Raise your hand toward them. It's a gesture, but it shows that you mean to bless and not to curse."

I extend my hand out.

"Open your palm toward them."

I open my palm toward the people who are still flashing by at the end of the spoke.

"Now bless all of them. Tell them all that you're sorry and bless them."

I repeat what Mr. O has told me to say, and then I see the spoke light up. I smile, truly glad for having replaced curses with blessings. Suddenly, from outside the Waiting Room, I hear my cheering section erupt all together in boisterous shouts and applause, "Go, Bob!"

# 25
# THE HOLY GAUNTLET

I AM IN THE Waiting Room, and all the spokes of my wheel are lit up. The whole room is bathed in the golden light emitted from the wheel.

"Congratulations, Bob!" Mr. O exclaims.

I nod and stare in awe at the golden light that seems almost alive.

I feel a sense of relief. Before I can do anything, I realize that my clothes—my favorite weekend jeans and T-shirt—which I have worn since setting foot in the Waiting Room, are changing. I watch as they somehow transform into *fine, white linen*.

"How is this happening?" I ask.

"Well, you have arrived, as it were. Your clothes are changed to garments that will never wear out and are more comfortable than even your, uh, favorite pair of jeans that you wore when you were on earth." He smiles. "Welcome home, Bob."

Suddenly a loud cheer erupts from outside the Waiting Room. As if on cue, the walls that have enclosed us disappear, revealing lush vistas that stretch in all directions.

With my eyes wide in amazement, I ask, "Is this heaven?"

"Only a small part of it, but yes."

"One…two…three…well done, Bob!" the cheering section calls out in perfect unison.

Now they are coming forward to greet me. I'm surrounded by those who have been with me since the first spoke on my wheel went from darkness to light—my ancestors. I'm surrounded by men and women who are radiating what can only be described as holiness. Their eyes are shining with love and acceptance. Every expression is one of joy for me, for them, for one another. I am overwhelmed by what is happening.

My ancestors are gathered around, and I'm enjoying talking to each of them. In their midst I can see what must be angels freely mingling with them. They are different from us; they are taller and more muscular, and their eyes burn with a holy love.

I'm talking to one of my ancestors who lived hundreds of years ago. I had no idea he even existed, and now we are conversing in a universal language, a dialect I somehow know instantly. I wonder how this is possible. Everything has changed so drastically since the last spoke on my wheel was lit up.

I continue my conversation with this man. His name is Robaire, which is the same as mine, Robert—only in French. We both laugh.

I ask him, "So where did you live?"

"I lived in northern France near what is now called Normandy. Interestingly your grandfather, who was involved in WWII, landed on the beach where I spent many happy hours as a boy. What a coincidence."

"I never knew him. He passed away when I was very young."

"I know, but he's here. Would you like to meet him?"

"Of course!"

I see a man walking toward me. I recognize him from the pictures in our family album. I call out instinctively, "Grandpa?"

"Just call me Ernie," he says, beaming. "Here on my white stone, there is another name—my real name—but for now Ernie will do."

I hurry toward him and give him a bear hug. As I do so, all my ancestors form two lines, one on each side of us, leaving a pathway down the middle. Everyone grows quiet, smiling at me.

My grandfather looks at me and asks, "Are you ready to walk the *holy gauntlet*?"

I can see my lineage stretching out before me. Some are dressed as I am in fine, white linen, while others are wearing their period clothing.

I look at Ernie, my grandfather, and somehow know what to do. I smile and say, "Let's go."

Ernie takes my arm, and we slowly walk down the *holy gauntlet*. I hear voices in my head. They are speaking the new language I have just learned. They introduce themselves as we walk by. Some extend their hand in greeting. Others pat me on the back as I walk by. Still others are weeping, but these are tears of joy. Somehow no one speaks over one another. A warm sensation runs through my body, my mind, my spirit. For the first time in my life, I feel—what does Mr. O always say?—*whole, hale, and hearty.*

These are my *ancestors*—those who went before me, my kin, my blood, my progenitors—people I never could have known because there were no records, and everyone was lost in the darkness of death and time. But now everything has changed. We are restored in almost indescribable ways.

The *holy gauntlet* extends into the distance, and I realize I could spend eternity meeting and talking to all these people. Then I realize I *do* have eternity to meet and greet all these people!

Suddenly Ernie stops. I see all the people spread out, forming several lines. They are looking behind me at where I just came from—from what was the Waiting Room. Ernie motions to me to turn around, so I do.

There is Mr. O, standing perhaps one hundred feet away

from me. There's no mistaking him with his wild white hair and glasses.

At the same time, as if a hidden conductor has waved his baton, the crowd says in unison, "*No flesh! No sin! No death! No sting! Hail to the King! Hail to the King! Hail to the King!*"

My eyes go back to Mr. O as I wonder who these people are talking about. Where is the King? I think the King must be Jesus, but He's not here. So if it's not Him, who can it be?

As I'm staring at Mr. O, he begins to light up, as if every pore in his body is emanating light. Everyone is transfixed, watching the spectacle. Through the light that has enveloped Mr. O, I see another image forming. He is different from Mr. O in every way. His eyes are like flaming fire, and on His head are many crowns. The light is fading slowly, but I can see that He is clothed in a robe with a crimson stain on its edges.

There He is!

I realize, without anyone telling me, that it is Jesus, the risen Savior—the One who bore the sins of all humanity, and the One I have been interacting with since I arrived at the Waiting Room!

"Hi, Bob!" He says, laughing as He comes toward me.

I am dumbfounded, shocked, tongue-tied, and in awe—all at the same time. I try to grasp this revelation. "But…"

"I know." He smiles. "But if I had just been Myself, we never would have gotten through the spokes. Mr. O is just one of My many disguises to help people light up their wheels. Do you know what Mr. O stands for?"

My relatives are gathered around us, eager to hear what He has to say.

"Do you remember when you first arrived? I entered the Waiting Room and introduced myself as Mr. Olam."

I nod.

"Well, El Olam is a Hebrew name for Me, and it's translated '*Eternal God, Ancient of Days.*' I certainly fit that description!"

The crowd laughs, and so do I.

Ernie nudges me. "We love this part! It's always the best."

Jesus asks me, "How are the new threads? By the way, you can still call me Mr. O if you want to."

I look at the linen clothes I am wearing, still wondering how I changed into them without changing into them. "They're the most comfortable clothes I've ever worn."

"Good," He replies. "I'll let our tailors know."

The crowd laughs again.

"I see you've been meeting with your relatives. This is always good, and I love being a part of it."

I nod again, trying to put my thoughts in order. "How can we understand one another?"

"Do you remember the story about the Tower of Babel?"

"Yes, but not in great detail."

The crowd moves closer; they're hanging on to every word.

Mr. O begins, "It's a long and very involved story, and I could spend a good amount of time here, but the short of it is this: The Fallen Ones had been banished in the flood of Noah."

"You mean the real Noah?"

Grandpa Ernie leans closer and whispers, "Shhh, don't interrupt."

Jesus laughs. "It's fine. But I'll give you the CliffsNotes version. As I said, the Fallen Ones were banished along with their unholy offspring, the Nephilim. However, mankind reproduced, and soon the earth was once again like the days of Noah. Mankind wanted the power and technology that the Fallen Ones had given them, so they constructed a tower to bring the Fallen Ones back, to open the gateway—a portal. This is when *We* intervened. We saw what was going on, and *We came down to see the mischief for ourselves*."[1]

Grandpa Ernie nudges me again. "He means the Father, the Holy Spirit, and of course Himself."

"Thank you, Ernie," Mr. Olam says. Warm laughter comes from the crowd.

Ernie bows.

"As I was saying, We came down and saw what was going on. Our countermove to what the Dragon was up to was to confuse the language of the people. Up to that time, everyone spoke the same language, so Babel was just that—we confused the languages. However, the heavenly language is used here, and everyone knows it instantly. Everything is made new; everything is restored."

The crowd erupts in, "Hail to the King!"

Jesus steps toward me, and Ernie moves away slightly to allow Him to come closer. "I have something to tell you, Bob."

"What?"

"Not here and not right now, but turn around and take a good look at your family." He pauses for a moment and then adds, "And say goodbye."

I am confused. I just got rid of all the dark spokes on my wheel, and now I have to say goodbye? "I don't understand."

"Trust Me. That's all you have to do."

At this point Grandpa Ernie gives me a hug, and my relatives crowd around me. Some are crying, others are smiling with a knowing look, and a few are hugging me, saying, "*We'll see you again real soon.*"

The crowd disperses, leaving just Jesus and me alone. He looks at me and asks, "Are you ready?"

I have no idea what being "ready" is at this point, and before I can say anything, somehow we have jumped through time and space and are standing alone on a beach. The white sand stretches out forever, scattered with clusters of palm trees. The water is calm, and I can hear a faint lapping of the waves as they caress the shoreline. It appears to be night because I see a moon-like light above us, making the ocean shimmer with silver, but it's much larger than any moon I have ever seen. It's so peaceful and serene that I want to stay here forever.

In a hushed tone, I ask, "Where are we?"

"Another part of heaven." He pauses, becomes very serious, and then begins again. "This will be hard for you to understand. But you're not the first person this has happened to, and it's not a mistake, so please don't think you've failed in any way because you haven't."

I bite my lower lip, not knowing how to react to what He's saying.

"I'm going to send you back."

"Back where? Earth?"

He nods. "You're not finished there quite yet, and what you went through in the Waiting Room is to prepare you for what's next. You have a clean slate; you have done the work. Now you can go back and help others."

I think about this for a moment. "But I don't want to go back!"

Jesus nods knowingly. "No one ever wants to go back." He chuckles. Then His face grows solemn. "When you go, you take with you a part of heaven, an anointing that few people in all history have had. You will have a gifting, and you will bring healing to people."

I really can't believe what I'm hearing. In the distance two figures are coming toward us, and they are flying right above the sandy beach—angels. I realize they have wings, but when they land about twenty feet from where I'm standing, the wings somehow fold into their bodies. They are powerful men with fiery eyes and muscular torsos. They are taller than I am, and I am in awe.

"Don't be afraid," Jesus says, "and don't be intimidated by them."

I nod silently.

"They are here to take you back to earth, to put you back into your body. You will see things along the way that will shock you, but don't fear. These guardians will see you through, and all will be well."

I am very apprehensive at this point. I'm not sure why this is happening, but I trust what Jesus is saying, and angels will escort me through...what? I can only imagine.

Jesus comes close and wraps His strong arms around me.

Tears run down my face. "I don't want to go."

"You trust Me, right?

"Yes."

"Remember this: I will be with you wherever you go—even unto the end of the age."

He releases me, and the two angels are suddenly by my side.

One of them says, "Hold on!" Before I can do or say anything else, they have grasped me under my arms, their wings unfold, and we are flying to...where? I can only imagine.

# 26
# FINAL DESTINATION

I AM FLYING THROUGH an unknown space, rocketing toward what I assume to be earth as my final destination, although I don't see anything that resembles it yet. The two angels have me in a "bubble" like the one around me when I went into the Escape Tunnel to get Aunt Mary. But this bubble is created by the angels, and the light coming from their bodies somehow seems alive. We are heading down and then up. I can see what appear to be stars and other angels flying in the distance. It has become dark—very dark—and suddenly a feeling of great dread overcomes me.

"Look away," one of the angels tells me. "Shield your eyes. You don't need to see this." He draws his sword. From its tip a brilliant beam of light shoots out and illuminates what is in front of us. I can't help but look, and to my horror I see dark, grotesque figures flying out of our way. They are hideous. Their dark, twisted faces are snarling at us as they bare their teeth, like the fangs of a lion. It is beyond nightmarish.

"Shield your eyes!" the angel admonishes me strongly, so I shut my eyes and tuck my face into the angel's side.

I moan, recalling the horror I have just seen.

"You will not remember this. You will be free from it," the other angel says in a comforting voice.

We continue to fly for a while, and then we slow down.

"You can open your eyes now," an angel informs me.

We are hovering high above earth in space. I can see the blue sphere with its continents and oceans, and I am rendered speechless. I think the angels have paused here deliberately so I can gather myself.

I ask them, "Where did we just come from? It was terrifying."

"We have come through the *second heaven*, a place where the Dragon resides with all his evil minions. It is his domain, at least for now. But soon we will fight against him, remove him from there, and cleanse it from all the foul things that have taken place there for millennia."

I shudder, but one of the angels places his hand on my head, and I feel like I am being supernaturally cleansed from what I just saw.

He continues, "Humans were not made to look at the things that dwell in the second heaven, and yet some take concoctions to intentionally place themselves there to gain power."

I shake my head. "I don't know what you're talking about."

The other angel says, "After the fall of man in the garden, some of the Dragon's legions were sent to earth. Some of these were *Watcher angels.* The Watcher angels left their first estate, heaven, and when they came to earth, they taught mankind forbidden things. One of those forbidden things was the cutting of roots to make potions, enabling a human soul to detach from its body and go to the second heaven to gain what is foolishly called wisdom and knowledge. This has been practiced through the millennia of your earth time. However, this knowledge and wisdom come with a price—that price is your soul."

I nod, but I still don't really understand all that is being said.

The angel continues, "What you call shamans or occultists on earth have been accessing the second heaven for millennia and continue to do so even to this day. But, as I told you, soon it will end."

We move again; this time we're headed down toward earth.

Suddenly we are back in the hospital room. I can see Evelyn, Phil, and Marsha. I can see my dead body on the hospital bed, and a sheet is covering my face. A nurse is unhooking me from the monitors. Pastor Fred is there too. He's trying to console Evelyn, but she is sobbing bitterly.

I ask the angels, "They can't see us, can they?"

"No, nor can they hear us."

Phil is holding his cell phone in his hand, but his head is lowered, and I can see he is trying to cope with my death.

Marsha is staring at the floor with a blank look on her face. She has been crying, and an unlit cigarette dangles limply from her lips.

"You have to go back into your body," one angel tells me.

"We'll help you," the other angel adds.

Before I can say anything, they have picked me up, and somehow I feel myself in my body! I open my eyes, take a deep breath, and sit straight up in the hospital bed. The sheet covering my face falls away.

Evelyn screams and collapses in Pastor Fred's arms, her cry echoing through the room.

Phil jumps to his feet with a look of bewilderment, steps toward me, and freezes, staring at me wide-eyed. "Dad?"

A nurse runs into the room, takes one look at me, and her jaw drops. She runs back out of the room, yelling, "*Doctor! Doctor! Doctor!*"

"Bob?" Fred's face is ashen, and his eyes are bulging out of his head.

"It's me," I reply, adjusting myself in the bed.

Evelyn is just coming to when she sees and hears me and then faints again.

Marsha bolts up in her chair, the cigarette falling to the

floor, as she announces, "No way!" She runs frantically out of the room, where she collides with a nurse carrying a tray. Everything goes flying in disarray and noisy commotion.

"Bob?" Fred asks again, rubbing his eyes and squinting at me. "Bob?"

A doctor and two nurses run into the room.

"Mr. Frisbee? Mr. Frisbee?" One of the nurses looks at me in utter disbelief.

The doctor tries to get through the clamor. "Mr. Frisbee, uh, you've been dead for over an hour. How…how…"

"I'm here! *How long* have I been gone?"

Another doctor comes running over and grabs my arm, checking my pulse.

"You flatlined over an hour ago. You were clinically dead. I know because I tried to bring you back and couldn't."

"Dad," Phil blurts out, "you were dead!"

Marsha is standing in the doorway, stunned. "Dad, we all saw it. You were dead. We all saw it!"

"His pulse is good," one doctor says.

Evelyn comes around, picks up her head, and looks at me, blinking. "Bob?"

"Yes, it's me, Evie. I'm here, and I love you. Sorry for the surprise."

"Surprise?" Marsha says. "I'll say. The surprise of a lifetime!"

The other doctor has his stethoscope on my chest, listening. "Heartbeat is good and regular."

"Dad, you were dead!" Phil says.

"*Really* dead," Marsha adds. "You stopped breathing."

Fred chimes in. "The doctors couldn't bring you back."

"They said *massive* heart failure," Evelyn adds.

Fred looks at the doctors and asks, "How is this possible?"

Both doctors shake their heads with nothing more to offer.

I point to the angels and ask, "Don't you see my companions?" Everyone looks to where I'm pointing.

Phil says, "Dad, there's nothing there but the wall." A confused look creases his face.

"You don't see them," I ask again, "the angels?"

The doctors look at each other.

"Angels?" Pastor Fred asks, looking at the wall where the angels are, but I can tell he doesn't see them.

"They're right there," I insist. I look over, and one of the angels waves at me and then points upward. I can tell they're getting ready to leave.

I nod and say to them, "Thank you for everything." With that they vanish through the ceiling.

"Take it easy, Mr. Frisbee," one of the doctors cautions. "You've had a very dramatic medical emergency that we're still trying to figure out."

I smile at the doctors. "They just left."

Fred leans toward me. "Who just left?"

"The angels. You didn't see them? They brought me back. I didn't want to, but here I am."

"Dad, are you OK?" Marsha asks as she and Phil come closer to my bed.

"Never better. Why are you asking?"

"You were dead, Dad," Marsha declares. "D.E.A.D.! Deader than a doornail…dead."

"You were toast, Dad," Phil adds.

"Maybe I was *mostly* dead," I quip, using the line from the movie *The Princess Bride* that Phil and Marsha watched countless times when they were young.

"This isn't funny, Dad," Phil protests. "You weren't *mostly* dead; you *were* dead. We all witnessed your last breath."

"Mom was hysterical," Marsha adds.

Evelyn sounds exhausted. "Bob, I can't believe—you're alive."

I swing my legs over the edge of the hospital bed and grab her hand. "I'm here, Evie, and I'm 100 percent alive and well. I'm not planning on dying again anytime soon."

Evelyn grabs my hand and kisses it as she starts crying.

"Take it easy, Mr. Frisbee," one of the docs admonishes again.

"Doc, I'm OK. You checked my vitals, and everything is normal. So am I good to go?"

"What?" Phil exclaims. "Dad, you were clinically dead for over an hour!"

"Well, miracles do happen," I quip.

"Miracles? There are no such things as miracles," Marsha snaps.

"Miracles?" Fred asks, paying closer attention.

I smile at all of them. "Yes, I'm a walking miracle, because I was dead, and now I'm alive again. How do you explain that?"

Fred turns to the doctors. "Have you ever seen anything like this?"

They both shake their heads.

"How do you explain this?" Fred asks. "Do you have any answers?"

The doctors look at each other, and the room goes silent.

One doctor says, "We've heard of things like this before, but usually the patient is dead for only a few minutes—perhaps ten minutes. But we've never seen someone come back to life after being dead for over an hour."

"An hour and eighteen minutes to be exact," one of the nurses adds.

I press them for an answer. "So it's a miracle then?"

"I don't believe in miracles," one of the doctors mumbles.

"Then how do you explain me?"

"Yeah, how do you explain my dad coming back to life?" Marsha asks, looking at the doctors and folding her arms across her chest.

Both doctors stare at the floor uncomfortably, and then one of them mumbles, "We don't know."

"Then maybe we're witnessing a miracle," Evelyn says, hesitantly.

"Bingo!" I exclaim.

"I never thought I would see a real miracle." Pastor Fred exhales, shaking his head.

"Well, this is your first. Congrats!" I declare. "Hey, I'm really hungry. What do you have to eat around here?"

"Get Mr. Frisbee something," one of the doctors says to a nurse, who then scurries out of the room.

A group of nurses, doctors, and administrators crowd the hallway, peering into my room. I wave at them. "I'm a walking miracle!"

They laugh and applaud.

"I'm alive!" I announce as I stand up for the first time.

"Easy, Mr. Frisbee," one of the doctors warns.

I jump up in the air and click my bare feet together, offering some proof of my recovery.

"Easy does it," he says again, nervously.

Everyone outside the room cheers again, with more applause.

"Where are my clothes?"

"Dad, you're not leaving here!" Marsha scolds.

"Why not? My vitals are fine. And besides, I'm whole, hale, and hearty and ready to leave this place."

"I folded them here," Evie says as she gets up for the first time. She wraps her arms around me, and I can tell she doesn't want to let me go.

"I can't believe you're alive," she whispers through a smile.

I kiss her forehead. "As alive as you are, Evie."

"Let me get your things."

"Doc? Everything checks out, right? So can I leave?"

The two doctors look at each other, and one says, "Well, we can't hold you here against your will, and all your vitals check out. But we're still wondering how you came back to life."

"I told you, the angels. But there's so much more to the story, and this isn't the place to tell it."

"Bob, are you sure you're well enough to leave?" Evie asks, handing me my clothes.

"Yes. Let me get dressed, and then we'll get out of here."

"Are you sure about this, Bob?" Fred asks. "You saw angels?" he whispers.

"Yes, and I'll tell you all about it, but not here."

"Dad, are you *sure* you're OK?" Phil asks.

"Yeah, Dad, are you sure?" Marsha adds.

"I'll say it again. Whole, hale, and hearty. Better than ever."

I head toward the bathroom in my private hospital room, throw off the hospital smock, and get back into my favorite jeans and T-shirt. Then I open the door and say, "Let's go!"

"Bob, are you *sure* you're OK?" Evie asks again. "You could stay awhile longer."

"Not a minute more. I feel great. Let's get out of here. But first, I want to thank all of you who helped me before I died."

I shake the doctors' hands, and then, grabbing Evie's hand, we head to the door. I pat Phil on his back and give a light pat on Marsha's head. At the door the small crowd of people makes way. They're applauding again, *just as my ancestors did in the Waiting Room.*

My little family is gathered around me, as well as Pastor Fred, as we walk down the corridor toward the elevator. Nurses and doctors and others are still following us.

We get into the elevator, and I wave to the folks as the doors close. Fred presses the "L" button, and we head to the lobby.

The doors open, and our little group steps out onto the polished granite floor of the hospital lobby.

"This way." Fred points, and we head toward the entrance. "Once you get settled, we need to talk about this," he whispers.

I smile. "We will. There's a lot to talk about."

As we move toward the exit, my eyes catch something off to my left. To my astonishment there is Mr. O! He's dressed as a doctor, and He's carrying a large file under His arm. He lifts a finger to His lips and throws the file into the air. All the pages come flying out, turn into white doves, and fly toward the ceiling, where they disappear. Mr. O gives me a thumbs-up, and He vanishes. I realize that it was my file He was carrying, and that it's gone forever.

I stop and point to where Mr. O was. "Did you see Him?"

Evie looks at me. "See who?"

I realize I might be sounding a little short of a full deck, so I change the subject. "Nothing, just a trick of the light. Let's go."

I steer the group toward the main doors, and we emerge into warm sunlight. Taking a deep breath, I say, "It's good to be alive—again! I have so much more to do."

*To be continued...*

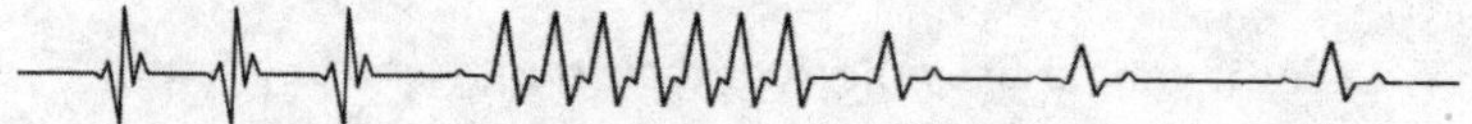

# FOR MORE INSIGHT

EVERAL THEMES AND concepts take center stage in this book that may need a little more explanation. Here they are, beginning with the most important one: forgiveness.

**Forgiveness**

These are words of the *Hero of Humanity* (Jesus Christ)—I got that title from the late author/minister/broadcaster Russ Dizdar. Some of you insist on one translation over another, but the Bible is very clear in every translation as to what Jesus means in Matthew 6:14–15. I've included just three translations of the passage that show this extraordinary teaching on forgiveness, and it is the nexus for this book, *The Waiting Room*.

> For if you forgive others their trespasses, your heavenly Father will also forgive you, but if you do not forgive others their trespasses, neither will your Father forgive your trespasses.
>
> —MATTHEW 6:14–15, ESV

> For if ye forgive men their trespasses, your heavenly Father will also forgive you: But if ye forgive not men

> their trespasses, neither will your Father forgive your trespasses.
>
> —Matthew 6:14–15, KJV

> For if you forgive others for their transgressions, your heavenly Father will also forgive you. But if you do not forgive others, then your Father will not forgive your transgressions.
>
> —Matthew 6:14–15, NASB

I think I made my point! Simply put, if we forgive, then we are forgiven; if we don't, we're in a heap of trouble.

The entire premise of *The Waiting Room* has to do with forgiveness. Bob has unforgiveness in his heart toward lots of people—just like you and me—but with the help of Mr. O, he begins to learn about forgiveness. Of course, if you're reading this, you know who Mr. O is!

Let me tell you a story. Thirty-five years ago, I was a worship leader at a church. There were problems there, and without getting into the nitty-gritty of it, I can only say we were run out of that church—*on a Sunday morning.* That was it. In fact, the pastor came up to me and stated, "I should just coldcock you right now!" Here is the offense that led to this very public expulsion.

While the pastor was in China on a missions trip, we had his wife up for dinner. She was our daughter Corrie's teacher. Mistake number one.

During dinner she confided in us about her marriage. I was taken aback. There were real problems. I never said anything to anyone else—I only called the head elder and said, "You need to deal with this."

Somehow, confidences were shattered, everything blew up, and we were escorted from the church grounds on Sunday morning. Six months later the pastor stepped down, divorced his wife, and married his wife's best friend. No one—not one person—ever called me. No one ever reached out. I was left without a church and abandoned by people who had become like family to us. I was appalled, hurt, broken, and despondent about the way we had been treated. I became bitter. I was mad at God, and two years went by.

One day while driving to work, the Holy Spirit spoke very clearly to me. It was the above passage. *If you don't forgive them, then your Father can't forgive you.* I repented immediately. It was a very sobering moment.

There are people who go to church every Sunday and follow all the rules, smile at everyone, put their tithe in the collection plate, and wear their Sunday best, yet they are bound by unforgiveness. They are in a prison of their own making. They lick their wounds, like I did, in self-justification. The wounds fester. The person feels justified, and in many cases, they are. But the overarching statement by Jesus, who is fully God and fully man, echoes through the ages with a dire warning.

*If we don't forgive, the Father can't forgive us.*

Remember, Jesus is on the cross. He is broken, pierced, humiliated, and naked as He hangs there. There is no coming down, there is no happy ending. Yet in the midst of His passion, He says this: *Father, forgive them, for they know not what they do.* This is what we look to as our model.

Incredible. He could have come down. He could have chosen not to go through with it, to not die—yet He did. *How do you kill God?* You can't. Yet He dies, and thus the price is paid for all of our sins. The only requirement is that we forgive those who have wounded us, whether it is our parents, siblings, relatives, bullies at school, abusive friends, abusive teachers—the list is endless. We are called to forgive. Period.

Here's something to think about. I am not stating that unforgiveness is the basis for all disease, but let's face it—it certainly can contribute to a range of ailments. It's not healthy physically, mentally, or spiritually. And as we see in the Scripture passage above, after a time it *will* separate us from the love of God.

There's a woman I have known for decades. She is a toxic blend of bitterness and unforgiveness. When you rattle her cage, a stream of profanities and curses issues forth with unrestrained unforgiveness.

Some of you who are reading this hold unforgiveness in your hearts. Drop it like you would a hot coal from a fire. Forgive. It's that simple. Just *light up your wheel* with the balm of forgiveness. Set yourself free from the prison, from the bondage you have placed upon yourself.

This simple prayer is a good place to start:

> *Father, I forgive those who have hurt me. I repent from the sin of unforgiveness. I ask that You set me free from the bondage I have taken into my soul and spirit. Thank You that You forgive me, and I will not pick this up again! It is finished, cleansed with the blood of Jesus. I choose to forgive.*

**Outer Darkness**

Please remember that this is a novel and I am taking some theological liberties throughout the book. When all is said and done, *The Waiting Room* is a work of fiction. I am using outer darkness as an illustration of what may happen to people who hold on to their unforgiveness. Remember, Jesus stated emphatically that unless we forgive those who "trespass against us," our Father cannot forgive us. Jesus' statement is very sobering, to say the least.

> But if you do not forgive others their trespasses [their reckless and willful sins, leaving them, letting them

> go, and giving up resentment], neither will your Father forgive you your trespasses.
>
> —Matthew 6:15, amp

While we don't know exactly what and where this outer darkness is, we can rely on Scripture that it is a place devoid of the presence of God. Jesus references it in Matthew 22:13. I am using *outer darkness* to illustrate the gravity of unforgiveness in our hearts and how damaging it is to our spirits. I truly believe unforgiveness leads to bitterness, which can harden our hearts and minds and keep us from His presence. I think we can agree that outer darkness is a place none of us ever wants to set foot in.

**Souls Under the Altar**

The "souls under the altar" passage, found in Revelation chapter 6, has always intrigued me.

> Then I looked and saw a pale green horse. Its rider's name was Death, and Hades followed close behind. And they were given authority over a fourth of the earth, to kill by sword, by famine, by plague, and by the beasts of the earth. And when the Lamb opened the fifth seal, I saw under the altar the souls of those who had been slain for the word of God and for the testimony they had upheld. And they cried out in a loud voice, "How long, O Lord, holy and true, until You avenge our blood and judge those who dwell upon the earth?"
>
> —Revelation 6:8–10, bsb

When I read this, I can't help but complain, "Excuse me, can you please expound on this?" Who are these martyrs?

As you know from reading *The Waiting Room*, Bob has a problem with those who perished in the Holocaust, and frankly, so do I. Think about it: The Jews whose lives were taken from them are martyrs because they died for being Jews and nothing else. Are these the souls under the altar? In my opinion, anyone who was put to death on either side of the "testaments"—the faithful believer in YHWH in the Old Testament or follower of Yeshua (Jesus) in the New Testament—is a martyr because their life was taken from them for no other reason than their faith.

I know some of you will disagree, and that's fine, but that's what I'm going with. He loves us. God is love, and in Him is no darkness at all.

**My Stance on Suicide**

What is the unpardonable sin? The Bible isn't exactly clear. Some would posit that it's blaspheming the Holy Spirit, and I'm leaning in this camp.

I want to make it clear that in no way am I suggesting that suicide is acceptable. It is not—all life is precious, from the moment of conception to the last breath. However, I do not believe that suicide is the unpardonable sin.

Here's a good link that expounds upon this: https://www.billygraham.ca/answer/is-suicide-the-unpardonable-sin/.

**Near-Death Experiences (NDEs)**

I had an NDE years ago when I was hospitalized with a fever over 106. Two beings came and took me up and then dropped me into different places. The first place was like a yellow desert, and in the distance I could see life forms that were coming for me. I didn't like it, and once I decided that I wanted to leave, the beings came and got me, and we went up to another place.

This second place was like a gambling casino. I found myself at a table throwing dice, and I was winning. The people around me were cheering me on, but when I looked at them out of the corners of my eyes, they were like zombies. Their flesh was green, and I could see their skulls.

I ran out of there, and then the two beings came and got

me again, and up we went. Next, they dropped me off in this beautiful mansion. I felt at home there, and it was good until I realized there were no other people around. I felt lonely, so once again the two beings came and got me.

This time we went up and up and up, and they let me down in a beautiful garden. Every flower was singing its own song. It was the most beautiful place I have ever seen. I had a feeling that other people would come and get me. I was on top of a mountain, and to my right was a waterfall. In the distance was a beautiful valley. Then I had the sensation of falling, and I awoke in a bed in the hospital three days after being admitted there. A nurse with red hair stood beside my bed, and when I saw her, I asked her if she was an angel.

In our *Watchers* series, Richard Shaw and I interviewed a man who was an atheist. But after having a near-death experience in which he spent time with Jesus, he became a believer and later became a pastor. I'm speaking of Howard Storm. He was rescued by Jesus and then sent back. I would encourage you to watch the interview in *The Best of Watchers*. That interview with Howard was amazing.

To access the DVD, scan the QR code or visit https://tinyurl.com/bdcufyy9.

Here's something to think about (I got this from my good friend Matt Brunet). Howard was sent back. I was sent back. But what about the people who aren't sent back? We don't hear from them because they remain on the other side. With that in mind, I realize what I'm about to say will ruffle a lot of theological feathers. What if, like Howard, people are given one last chance? They see Jesus. I'll say it again: God is love, and He doesn't want anyone to perish. Those people who still reject Him and do so by their own choosing wind up in outer darkness. I know some of you will want to write to me and set me straight, but if we're honest, it's a mystery at best.[1]

### The White Horse Police Force

> And the armies in heaven, clothed in fine linen, white and clean, followed Him on white horses.
>
> —REVELATION 19:14, NKJV

This is one of my favorite scriptures. We are in heaven with Jesus, and we are on white horses. We are riding down to earth to watch the King destroy the armies that are set against Him. (See Psalm 2.) He destroys them by the sharp sword that goes from His mouth. In my opinion, Jesus just stops holding them together.

Think about Colossians 1:17: "And He is before all things, and in Him all things hold together."

In my opinion, Jesus stops holding those armies that are set against Him together. They just collapse on the field of battle and bleed out.

So here we are with Jesus. We see Him land on the Mount of Olives, splitting it in two. There will be about four billion people left on the earth. Everyone is watching via the internet, satellite hookups, and cell phones. People are thinking, "Who is this Man on the white horse?"

This is where we come in. He dispatches us throughout the cities on the earth. We preach the gospel, we heal the sick, we raise the dead. We do greater works than He did when He was on earth.

That's my hope, and when I think about it, I tingle all over.

I can't wait for my white horse, and these horses can fly! Think about that!

To read about humor in the Bible and my thoughts on Beethoven giving concerts in heaven (and especially *Für Elise*), scan the QR code or visit LAMarzulliBooks.com/waiting/resources.

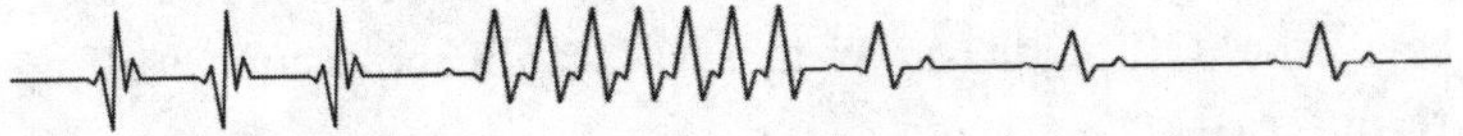

# THE STORIES BEHIND THE STORY

SOME OF THE stories in this book are inspired by real events. To hear me share the journey that inspired certain moments in *The Waiting Room*, scan the QR code or visit LAMarzulliBooks.com/waiting/resources.

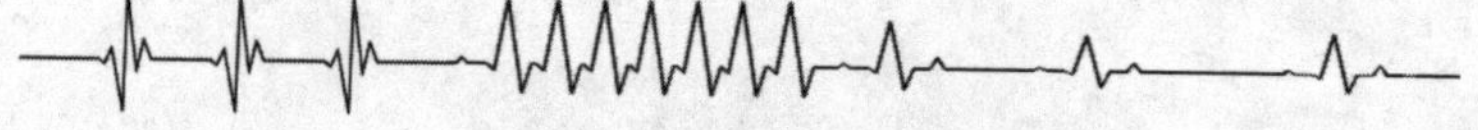

# DAILY PRAYER FOR STRENGTH, GUIDANCE, AND FOCUS

*For I am a man (or woman) chosen by God, ordained by Him, and set apart for His purposes, for a time such as this.*

*It is He who guides my steps.*

*It is He who sets my feet on paths of His choosing.*

*He is my strength, my shield, my rock.*

*The blood of Jesus, who is the Lamb of God that takes away the sins of the world, cleanses me from all my sin.*

*I have made a covenant with my eyes, and I am faithful to the wife (husband) of my youth.*

*I am a loving husband (wife).*

*I protect and love my children.*

*My hand is on the plow with my work, and I will not look back.*

*I have compassion and love for everyone I come in contact with, as I am the Lord's ambassador to that person.*

*I will pray for those who persecute me and forgive those who trespass against me.*

*When I am triggered by circumstances in life that bring up old patterns of behavior, I will not succumb to them. I will lean in and look toward the keeper of my soul...Jesus.*

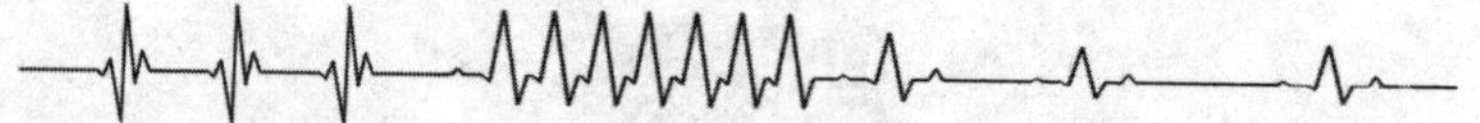

# A PERSONAL INVITATION FROM THE AUTHOR

GOD LOVES YOU deeply. His Word is filled with promises that reveal His desire to bring healing, hope, and abundant life to every area of your being—body, mind, and spirit. More than anything, He wants a personal relationship with you through His Son, Jesus Christ.

If you've never invited Jesus into your life, you can do so right now. It's not about religion; it's about a relationship with the One who knows you completely and loves you unconditionally. If you're ready to take that step, simply pray this prayer with a sincere heart:

> *Lord Jesus, I want to know You as my Savior and Lord. I confess and believe that You are the Son of God and that You died for my sins. I believe You rose from the dead and are alive today. Please forgive me for my sins. I invite You into my heart and my life. Make me new. Help me walk with You, grow in Your love, and live for You every day. In Jesus' name, amen.*

To hear me personally share about what it means to follow Christ, scan the QR code or visit LAMarzulliBooks.com/waiting/resources.

If you just prayed that prayer, you've made the most important decision of your life. All of heaven rejoices with you, and so do I! You are now a child of God, and your journey with Him has just begun. Please reach out to my publisher at pray4me@charismamedia.com if you accepted Jesus today or if this book has encouraged or impacted your life in any way. We'd love to celebrate with you and send you free materials to help strengthen your faith. We look forward to hearing from you!

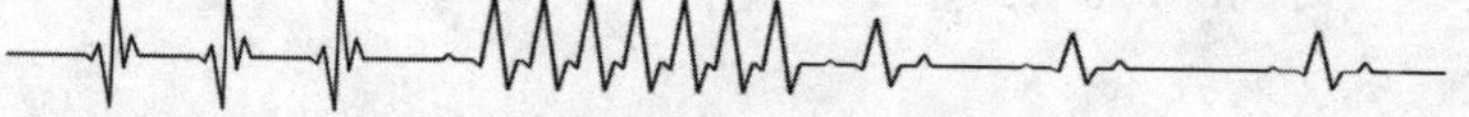

# NOTES

### Chapter 9

1. Luke 23:34.

### Chapter 10

1. Revelation 19:11, 12–13.
2. Revelation 19:14.
3. Revelation 19:15.

### Chapter 11

1. See Revelation 21:4.
2. John 1:29, ESV.
3. See Genesis 3:15.

### Chapter 12

1. See Genesis 3:5 and John 10:10.
2. Romans 8:28, KJV.
3. See 2 Samuel 12:23.
4. John 1:1.
5. 1 Corinthians 15:51–53, KJV.

### Chapter 13

1. John 1:5, KJV.

### Chapter 15

1. Revelation 21:4.
2. Zechariah 12:10, KJV.
3. Exodus 20:4, KJV.

### Chapter 16

1. Romans 8:28, KJV.

### Chapter 17

1. Luke 23:34, KJV.

### Chapter 18

1. Revelation 21:8, NKJV.

### Chapter 19

1. Revelation 19:11–14.
2. Revelation 19:14.

### Chapter 21

1. See Genesis 3:15.

### Chapter 23

1. Romans 12:14.

### Chapter 25

1. See Genesis 11:5–6.

### For More Insight

1. See Billy Hallowell, "Boy Who Says He Nearly Died, Visited Heaven Speaks Out Decades After 'Heaven Is For Real' Journey," CBN, June 1, 2025, https://cbn.com/news/world/boy-who-says-he-nearly-died-visited-heaven-speaks-out-decades-after-heaven-real-journey.

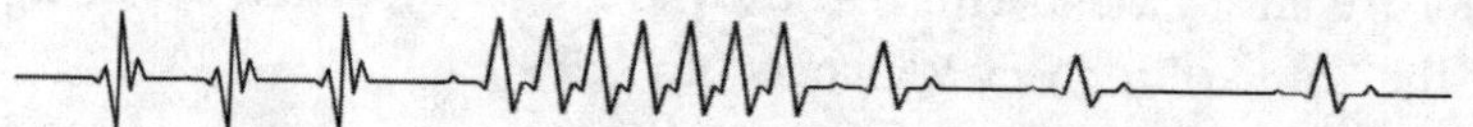

# SPECIAL THANKS

I WOULD LIKE TO take a moment to thank many people who have impacted me throughout my life. Part of me wants to thank anyone I've ever had contact with, even for the briefest of time, like meeting someone at a bus stop, you talk for a minute, and then the bus comes and you never see them again! It may seem inconsequential, but I am convinced that every person we come in contact with can impact us in ways that may seem trivial at the time but add up to a greater purpose, especially for those of us who follow the Lord. He has a way of inserting a person in our lives at just the right moment. With that said, I want to take the time to thank some of the people who have impacted my life, enriched it in priceless ways, and left a lasting legacy on my soul and spirit.

Peggy Marzulli, my "Wifey" of forty-one years, who has been a constant source of unconditional love and inspiration—you get a special reward in heaven for putting up with me!

Corrie Marzulli-Hicks, John Adam Hicks, Opal Hicks, Sarah Marzulli and friend David Mendoza, Tony Marzulli, and Claudia Wellington

Special thanks to my editor, friend, and sister in Christ, Sanda

Allyson. You are amazing! You hold my feet to the fire and cheer me on to the finish line. Thank you for all you do.

Special thanks to Gil Zimmerman.

To all my wonderful friends who are brothers and sisters in the Lord at Prophecy Watchers (my tribe!):

- My elder brother, friend, and confidant, Gary Stearman, and his wife, Doris
- My good friend who is always a phone call away, Bob Ulrich, and his wife, Krissie
- My brother in all our ongoing Nephilim adventures, Mondo Gonzales, and his wife, Angela
- Tyler Wood, the great director behind the cameras at Prophecy Watchers
- Dave and Lisa Boswell, Josiah and Lauren, Josh and Christina Peck, Larry and Loretta Ollison, Pastor Matt and Randi Freeman, Brad and April Brady, Don Mercer
- All the women who package the material and greet callers—you do a great job!

Thanks to all those who have blessed us financially through the years, especially Bart Krulic, J and G, Loy Fox, and Gail Clark.

Vicki Joy Anderson and Karin Wilkenson, two wonderful friends and authors we are proud to publish!

All the incredible brothers and sisters at Charisma Media, including John Matarazzo, Debbie Marrie, Adrienne Gaines, Josh Nolette, Chad Dunlap, Kayla Mendez, Lisa Rae McClure, Angie Kiesling, and Makena Song.

Special thanks to Stephen and Joy Strang for believing in me.

All the folks I have interviewed over the years, who are too numerous to name here. I thank you for allowing me into your life.

Special thanks to the Colorado Prayer Group: Ruth Carroll, Bob Pietrzyk (Ski Buddy Bob!), Cindy Meinders, Maarten Meinders, Nancy Gunow, Cheryl Newey, Cindy Brandel, and Jeannie Belli.

Thank you to Matt and Yvonne Brunet for their friendship. It was Matt who pointed out to me the concept that people who have near-death experiences sometimes come back—but what about those who don't "come back"?

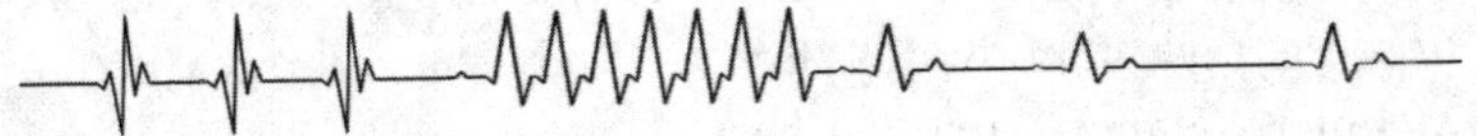

# ABOUT THE AUTHOR

UTHOR L.A. Marzulli is a lecturer/filmmaker/writer who has penned fifteen books, including *The Nephilim Trilogy*, which made the CBA bestsellers list.

Based on his work on the trilogy, Marzulli received an honorary doctorate from his mentor, Dr. I.D.E. Thomas, who was provost at Pacific International University. He was also honored with the Gold Medallion award from Chuck Missler at the K-House conference in 2014.

His book series *On the Trail of the Nephilim*, volumes I and II, reveals startling evidence of a massive cover-up of what he believes to be the remains of the Nephilim, the giants mentioned in the Bible.

Marzulli teamed up with film producer Richard Shaw to create *The Watchers* series, which grew to an eleven-episode catalog. One of those installments, *Watchers 7: UFO Physical Evidence*, won both the UFO Best Film and People's Choice Award at the UFO Congress in 2014.

With the passing of Richard Shaw, Marzulli teamed up with Gil Zimmerman, and the two have completed ten films in their ongoing UFO series. This is the only film series that deals with the many facets of the UFO phenomenon.

Marzulli is a frank "supernaturalist" who lectures on the subjects of UFOs, the Nephilim, and ancient prophetic texts, presenting his exhaustive research at conferences and churches and through all media platforms. He has been interviewed on numerous national and international radio and television programs.

For more information, scan the QR code or visit linktr.ee/l.a.marzulli.